Praise for Maggie Casper's *California Cowboy*

Rated 5 "First off, let me tell you this is one very hot read!"

~ *Tina, Ck's Kwips & Kritiques*

Rated 5 Blue Ribbons "CALIFORNIA COWBOY is a prime example of why fans eagerly anticipate each new story..."

~ *Chrissy Dionne, Romance Junkies*

Rated 4.5 "Maggie Casper tells a delightful story with sex hot enough to curl your toes..."

~ *Alisha, Two Lips Reviews*

California Cowboy

Maggie Casper

A Samhain Publishing, Ltd. publication.

Samhain Publishing, Ltd.
577 Mulberry Street, Suite 1520
Macon, GA 31201
www.samhainpublishing.com

California Cowboy
Copyright © 2007 by Maggie Casper
Print ISBN: 978-1-59998-785-9
Digital ISBN: 1-59998-205-6

Editing by Sarah Palmero
Cover by Dawn Seewer

First Samhain Publishing, Ltd. electronic publication: July 2007
First Samhain Publishing, Ltd. print publication: May 2008

Dedication

To Uncle William and Aunt Pearl who have worked, lived and loved on the real Lazy B Ranch for the last fifty years. I can't wait for my next visit. Thank you for the memories. I love you both!

Chapter One

Clay Bodine dragged himself up the stairs of the Lazy B Ranch, pushing open the front door with a weary shove. It had been a long, hard day and he was more than ready for a hot meal and an even hotter shower.

The smell of garlic and tomatoes hit him in a wave. It had to be Italian, and the scent permeated the air around him, making his stomach rumble.

He was a bit surprised that his younger brother, Chance, would take the initiative and cook supper. Hell, neither one of them could cook for beans, so Clay had already planned on cold sandwiches or something similar until tomorrow. He knew he'd miss Mildred. The woman was more like family than a housekeeper and cook. He just didn't realize how much until he and Chance spent several days in a row eating cold suppers. Now he couldn't wait for her to come back from visiting her daughter.

Grateful for a hot meal, Clay stripped as he climbed the stairs. When he was down to just his jeans, he grabbed a towel and headed to the end of the hall only to find the bathroom door locked, the sound of running water clear through the thick wood barrier.

"Damn," he mumbled, heading back toward the stairs. Clay wasn't sure he wanted to eat whatever Chance had fixed them if he'd done it before showering. There were all sorts of dirt and grime a cowboy could collect by the end of a hard day's work, and he sure as hell didn't want any of it near his food.

He was making his way to the downstairs bathroom when he heard the clang of pots followed by soft humming coming from the kitchen. Curious, Clay took a detour through the dining room and stopped dead in his tracks on the kitchen threshold.

A plump, denim-clad backside swayed mesmerizingly in front of him. The hips were attractively rounded and kept him in a trance-like state while they moved enticingly back and forth. The sound coming from the other end of the creature was smooth and mellow.

Her hair was a fiery red and held haphazardly in place by one of those scrunchie things all the girls seemed to wear these days. There wasn't a thing smooth or refined about her hair. It looked more like a mentally challenged bird had tried to build a nest in it.

The stirring of his cock against the confines of his jeans jolted Clay out of his perusal of the woman in front of him. He wondered who she was and was a bit bemused to think he might have just been checking out a friend of Chance's. At the same time though, something about her made him a bit tense. Chance had never brought a woman home before. At least not one who would be staying, and this woman had permanent written all over her. She seemed way too comfortable in his kitchen, in his house.

"Who the hell are you?" he demanded, moving into the kitchen.

When the woman shrieked and dropped a pan of what appeared to be lasagna onto the kitchen floor, Clay realized he'd probably gone about that the wrong way. Instead of turning on him in a fit of rage, the woman ran to the sink and thrust her arm under a stream of water, at the same time saying...

"Bobbie. Bobbie Carlington. And you must be Clay. Chance has told me so much about you."

He recognized her name right away, only she was supposed to be a he. Clay scowled at the petite yet curvy woman and decided Chance had some explaining to do. It would have to wait though since there was a bright red spot blooming on Ms. Carlington's forearm.

"Oh hell! Let me see," he insisted, moving forward to help.

"I'm just fine, thanks. I don't think it'll blister, but I'm not sure we can salvage any of that," she said, pointing to the mess on the kitchen floor.

Kind of ironic, Clay thought. Looked like he'd be eating sandwiches for supper after all. She turned to him and rested her small hand on his bare arm as she showed him her burn. The contact sent a bolt of desire straight to his groin, causing it to tighten unmercifully. He swiveled, hoping she hadn't noticed the bulge in his pants, or his reaction to her.

"I'll get some salve for that," he said as he stalked from the room toward the bathroom. He was going to kill Chance when he finally got his hands on him. He remembered Chance talking briefly about hiring a kid named Bobbie but he'd automatically thought Bobbie to be a boy. There sure in the hell was nothing boyish about this Bobbie.

She had the most magnificent set of boobs he'd ever seen. They were large and round and real. There was nothing fake about them babies. They moved when she moved and even gave an extra jiggle when she stopped. Small was okay, and perky was nice. Hell, even fake would do in a pinch, but a pair of gals like the ones belonging to Bobbie Carlington were made for loving. The things he could do to them, to her, were probably illegal in many states.

He threw his towel down on the closed toilet seat, grabbed the burn ointment out of the medicine cabinet, and strode back into the kitchen where Ms. Carlington was now down on her hands and knees. He was sure he was wrong, but it didn't seem like she was cleaning the mess. It looked more like she was painting the floor with it.

"Oh shit, hot, hot, hot," she chanted quietly as she picked up a clump of the lasagna and threw it at the trashcan. Not one piece made it in the container, not that she cared, evidently, because she went right back to smearing it around.

"Here, let me do that." Clay lifted her by the waist until she stood on her feet, staring at him with wide, innocent eyes. They were as green as emeralds and huge on her pale face.

"Oh no, I couldn't let you. I made the mess, I'll clean it." She turned her back to him and started to drop to her knees.

His first reaction was of unrelenting arousal. If she'd been facing him, it would have been so easy to guide her hands to the buttons of his fly and then swiftly move on to the even better lesson of training her to suck his cock just how he liked.

The only problem was that his second reaction, one of anger at having his orders ignored, took over. Grabbing her by the belt loop, Clay yanked until she was back firmly on her feet.

"Hey! What the hell, buddy?" She was mad, her eyes flashing at him. At that moment he knew she was going to be trouble.

"Put this on your burn. Now," he commanded when she hesitated.

"Well you're just the bossy one, aren't ya?"

"That's right, darlin', and don't you forget it. I'm the boss, what I say goes and the sooner you realize that, the better off we'll be."

"Ya think so, huh?" she replied in a sarcastic voice as she left the room. Clay wasn't sure whether to laugh or go after her and spank her sassy ass.

၆၁

Bobbie headed into the living room, her anger mounting. There was no one to blame but herself. Chance had warned her Clay was a hard man, one used to getting his way. Only she'd not paid much attention to his words. After all, she was a nice person, friendly and easy to get along with. Why wouldn't the man like her? He didn't even know her.

Bobbie wasn't one to let her feelings show, mainly because she never let herself get close enough to anyone to have feelings one way or another. It was a concept she'd learned at an early age, the same reason she never planned to marry. There was no way she could see herself spending the rest of her life under the thumb of a man like her father. She shuddered at the thought.

On the other hand, she could very well give some thought to spending some time under Clay Bodine. Thumb or any other body parts would work just fine, she thought with a giggle. The man was handsome as hell, tall and dark. His chocolate-brown eyes were intense. His wavy brown hair seemed a bit unruly, but it gave him a rakish look, a look any woman in her right mind would do a double take for. And even if he was too dominant for her taste, it didn't matter because she planned on using her eyes, not her hands or her mouth, or her...

"All right! Get a grip, Bobbie," she said aloud, chastising herself for her lewd thoughts.

The front of her shirt was splattered with sauce and since she hadn't been shown to a room yet, Bobbie proceeded to rummage through her single large suitcase right there on the living room floor.

She'd just taken out a clean t-shirt when Chance made his way down the stairs.

"Hey, kiddo."

"Oh, hi." Bobbie looked up as she closed the zipper on her luggage. "There was a problem with supper. I need to go change real quick and then I'll figure something else out."

She climbed the stairs and made her way to the restroom at the end of the hall where Chance had told her it was.

With her fresh shirt on, Bobbie took a deep breath to calm her frazzled nerves, and then made her way back to the kitchen. She could hear the men talking but thought nothing of it until she walked through the doorway and the room went so quiet you could hear the proverbial pin drop.

"We'll finish this later," Clay said to Chance, a scowl on his face.

Bobbie couldn't help the flash of anger she felt. There was just something about Clay that seemed to bring out the worst in her. She seemed unable to stop the words before they tumbled from her mouth. "Real subtle. You want me to leave so you two gentlemen can finish talking about me?" She'd stressed the word gentlemen on purpose because in actuality, they were both acting like asses.

"Sorry, Bobbie," Chance said, his voice serious.

"No problem," she answered then turned to Clay, pinning him with her stare. "Thanks for cleaning up my mess." Thanking him was the last thing she wanted to do, but he had cleaned it up, so it was only right that she thank him.

"No problem," he said mimicking her answer to Chance. He held her gaze, never wavering. "Now, we need to figure something out for supper."

ဆ

Later that night, after cleaning up the mess they'd made preparing a second supper, Bobbie let herself out the front door and onto the porch. She realized she probably should have been more adamant when she'd told Chance she knew next to nothing about cooking and had no idea where to start when it came to cleaning a big house.

Her mom had always taken care of the house, and after the death of her parents she'd lived in a tiny studio apartment. If you could even call it that. It was smaller, more like a box than an actual room.

When she'd met Chance Bodine at a horse auction in Oklahoma, she'd immediately felt at ease with him. He was easy to talk to and extremely friendly. Yet at the same time, she could tell you wouldn't want him as an enemy. He could be ruthless when it came to business matters, as she'd had the opportunity to see first hand.

He'd wanted Lady, her mare. It had been a sad day for Bobbie, but she'd held on to her composure. Mac McQuinn, her boss, was selling out and moving. The McQuinn Stables had been a part of her hometown for as long as she could remember and now, all of a sudden, she not only had to deal with the sale of her horse, but the loss of her job. And then Chance came along.

The first time Chance had laid eyes on her he'd just stood there and stared. It had been very unnerving to be looked at like that. If anyone was aware of her flaws, it was Bobbie herself. Her hair was too red, her eyes too big, and God only knew she had more curves than one woman should be burdened with. But he'd talked to her, putting her at ease, and over the next few days they'd come to an agreement.

Bobbie was to travel with Lady from Oklahoma to California where she would have a job as a housekeeper, room and board included, and be able to ride Lady whenever she wanted. Knowing Lady would no longer belong to her had been hard, but being offered the chance of a lifetime as well as the option of staying with Lady was much more than she had ever hoped for. So she'd given up her studio apartment, transferred the address where she could receive her correspondence college courses, and headed west to sunny California.

"Hey, you okay?" a voice asked from behind her.

"What? Oh yeah, I'm fine, just a bit tired I guess," she answered Chance.

"Well then, let's get you settled in so you can get some rest. The days tend to start early around here." Chance opened the door for her and followed her in.

He grabbed her suitcase, lifting it as if it weighed nothing, and then proceeded up the stairs. The hardwood floors were spic-and-span clean, not a speck of dust in sight. The narrow carpet running the length of the hall was done in browns with some deep red interspersed—it was beautiful and made her wonder why the Bodines needed a housekeeper.

"Here you go, Bobbie," Chase opened the door and set her suitcase just inside.

"Thanks, and I'm sorry I made such a mess about supper. I'll try harder tomorrow, okay?" Try was all she could promise since there was no way she could turn into a chef overnight.

"No problem. I'll see you in the morning," he said and then moved down the hallway toward another door.

Bobbie entered the room and quietly closed the door behind her, which threw her into darkness. With one hand she held onto the knob so she wouldn't get lost in the dark, and felt around on the wall for the light switch with the other. When she finally found it, it sent a shockingly bright light throughout the room. She stood there for a moment, blinking back the harsh light until her eyes adjusted and she could see her new room.

The room was done in blues and was utterly feminine, making Bobbie wonder who it belonged to. The carpet was plush beneath her sandal-clad feet. She longed to take off her shoes and wiggle her toes across its surface but decided that would have to wait.

She noticed two other doorways, one on each side of the room. Bobbie did a real quick eeny, meeny, miny, moe to choose which door to investigate first. The one she chose didn't open into a closet as she had thought it would. Instead it opened into a full bathroom, a beautiful bathroom with a corner shower to die for. She could see the dual showerheads through the clear glass and a shiver of anticipation went through her at the thought of taking a shower in there. The thought of what a couple could do in a shower like that was enough to get her juices flowing. Or at least what she thought a couple could do. She'd read about it and had even seen a few movies, but at the ripe old age of twenty-one, Bobbie Carlington was still a virgin.

Bobbie pulled herself from her thoughts and once again studied the bathroom. It was almost as big as her old apartment. She laughed at the thought, but the reality of it made her uneasy. Why would she, the hired help, be given such a room? It made no sense for her to have a bathroom of her own when Clay and Chance obviously didn't have such a luxury in their own rooms. Nope, it made no sense at all, and until she found out if it was a mistake, she wasn't going to unpack a stitch of clothing.

Bobbie was just about to leave the room when her curiosity—a trait some called nosiness—lured her into seeing what was behind door number two. With a flick of her wrist and a swing of her arm, she flung the door open.

Before her, lying on his bed in all his glory, was a completely naked and very aroused Clay Bodine.

Chapter Two

Clay was lying on his bed with his back against the headboard, enjoying a jerk session to its fullest extent, when the door connecting his room to the one beside it swung open. In its wake stood a green-eyed vixen, the exact same one he'd been fantasizing about.

He'd thought of nothing but her beautifully large breasts for most of the evening and whacking off to thoughts of sliding his cock between those pale globes had seemed the best option. Getting caught at it wasn't on the agenda. The damned woman was a menace, he thought, as he reached for the sheet to cover his now flaccid shaft.

"Don't you know how to knock, woman!" he thundered at a pink-cheeked Bobbie.

"Uh, well...umm, I..." she stuttered in way of an explanation, her face crimson with embarrassment. She cleared her throat and tried again. "I just wanted to see where this door led."

"Well now you know. So if you wouldn't mind, could you..." He motioned with his hand for her to turn around and leave the way she'd come.

She did as asked but quickly turned back around, once again catching him off guard. "Oh, but I was wondering..." was all she got out before he lost what was left of his temper.

"Out dammit, now!" When she scurried to the door, he took a deep breath in hopes of calming his temper. "After I get dressed, I'll meet you downstairs."

It was all he could manage when what he really wanted to do was wring her sexy little neck and pound Chance into a bloody pulp. The dumb son of a bitch was too stupid for his own good. Why the hell would he put Bobbie in the master bedroom next to his but not bother to say a word about it to either of them?

"Whatever the reason, it had better be a good one," Clay growled as he zipped the fly of his jeans.

The loud bang of the door reverberating off of the walls accomplished exactly what he wanted. A bleary-eyed Chance, dressed in only a pair of white boxer briefs, came stumbling out of his room.

"What in the hell are you slamming doors for, Clay? I just fell asleep," Chance grumbled.

"Come on, you'll see," Clay answered. He was looking forward to his brother's embarrassment.

When the two of them reached the living room, Bobbie looked up from her spot on the couch. Her cheeks were still flushed, almost the color of her hair, which was now flowing around her shoulders in a disarray of curls. The fiery mass complemented her pale skin and the freckles dotting her nose gave her an impish look, making Clay want her all over again.

"This really isn't necessary, Mr. Bodine," Bobbie said, clearly not wanting him to relay to Chance what had transpired between them. "Just do something to block the doorway and I promise I won't bother you again."

"Yes, darlin', I think it is necessary and I'll take care of the door first thing tomorrow." Turning to Chance, Clay demanded, "Why in the hell didn't you say something to either of us when you showed Bobbie to the master bedroom?"

Clay watched as Chance's eyes widened, his gaze moving between the two of them. "I didn't think about it. Why?"

Clay looked to Bobbie, interested to see what she would say. She didn't disappoint him when she opened her mouth, nothing more than a strangled sound of embarrassment making its way out, before she quickly snapped it shut. She looked completely scandalized by the thought of telling Chance anything. If he wasn't so pissed off about being caught masturbating, he'd be laughing his ass off at the look on her face.

"What she's trying to say is that in her nosiness, she walked through the connecting door and caught me in a rather compromising position, all by myself."

Clay had trouble holding back his laughter when Chance turned to Bobbie. "You mean you caught him..." Chance couldn't say the words but had no trouble making a close-fisted pumping motion with his hand, which only made Bobbie's face turn a brighter shade of red.

"I think I'll be going to bed now." Her voice was quiet as she obviously struggled for dignity.

When she was safely out of the room Chance, unable to hold back any more, put his face in his hands and started laughing. "I can't believe she walked in on you jacking off. Oh man, that is too funny," his brother said as his laughter subsided.

"Yeah, and if that wasn't bad enough, Chance, you replayed the motion for her, and in your underwear to boot." Clay had his turn to laugh when Chance immediately got quiet. His brother looked down, taking in his state of undress.

"Well hell, Clay, you could have said something."

"Why, Chance? You didn't bother to say anything when you stuck her in the room next to me." It felt good to get the final word in the matter, but didn't help much when he thought about the fact that Bobbie Carlington would soon be sleeping all snug in the four-poster, king-sized bed only a few feet away from him. That thought was enough to set him back a bit.

He wondered with more than a little fascination what she slept in. Would she wear something that covered her every curve from head to toe or would she sleep in one of those little baby-doll nighties that barely covered her treasures? Clay couldn't help but wonder which he would like more. Being completely nude would serve a better purpose, but tiny scraps of satin and lace covering her strategically would be purely erotic.

Before he let his mind get too far ahead and drag his body along for the ride, Clay gave himself a mental kick in the ass. She might be gorgeous, but she was young and he would bet that she was fairly innocent. Although he doubted a woman of her age who looked the way she did would be a virgin. Most important though, was the fact that she was an employee at the Lazy B and there was nothing about a relationship with her that would be easy. Before he knew it, she'd be insisting on marriage and children and making changes in a house he was more than happy with as it stood. Nope, come hell or high water, Bobbie Carlington was off limits.

‰

When Bobbie woke up before dawn the following morning, she still couldn't get the vision of a nude Clay out of her head. His body was magnificently put together and although she'd never seen a naked man up close before, she imagined him to be well-endowed. Belatedly, Bobbie wished she had gotten a better look. Her surprise entrance had startled Clay, and he covered himself so quickly she didn't see much.

She dressed casually in a pair of jean shorts, a tank top and some sneakers. She'd gone to bed with wet hair so was left with an atrocious tangle to deal with this morning. Brushing it was useless unless she wanted to look like she'd stuck her finger in a light socket, so she parted it and braided it, wishing all the while that she'd been born with straight hair.

Breakfast was going to have to be something simple, something she knew how to make because the thought of asking either man for help was out of the question. She settled on scrambled eggs and toast because there wasn't much a person could do to mess that up. Or so she thought when she began. After dropping an egg on the floor, she wasn't so sure.

It wasn't until she'd cracked the last egg that she realized she'd inadvertently dropped a piece of the white shell into the bowl.

"Shit," she mumbled, not at all liking the way the morning was starting out. After fishing around for the shell with no success, Bobbie gave up and said a silent prayer that the piece of shell ended up on her plate and not Clay's or Chance's.

The last two pieces of extra dark toast were being buttered when the Bodine brothers made their way into the kitchen. They were both extremely good looking, but that was where all the similarities seemed to end. Where Chance was easy going and a bit laid back, Clay was rigid and used to ruling the roost.

"Morning," she said brightly, not looking either of them in the eye. Too much had happened in a short amount of time and she wasn't exactly sure how she was supposed to deal with it all.

"Smells good." Chance poured himself a cup of coffee. She watched as he took a sip, her gaze faltering at his slight grimace.

"Is there something wrong with it? I've never made coffee before but I could do it over if you told me how many scoops to use."

Damn, feeling useless sucked big time.

"No, it's fine. Just fine, a bit stronger than we're used to around here, but it'll do. Next time just use three of those scoops," he coaxed gently.

She knew he was being nice for her benefit, but Clay evidently had no qualms about speaking his mind.

"This stuff's thick enough to stand a fork in," he grouched, ignoring the quelling look Chance was giving him.

"Here." Bobbie snatched the cup from Clay's hand. The hot coffee inside sloshed over, scalding her fingers, but she didn't care. Close to tears, the pain diverted her attention, keeping her from crying.

It was an asinine thought. She hadn't cried since her parents funeral and hadn't gotten close enough to anyone since to care enough to cry, except Mac.

When she reached the sink, she tossed the black concoction down the drain and did the same with the rest of the pot. She rinsed it out, measured three scoops, set the pot back on the burner and hoped for the best. It was only then that she noticed the back of her hand and fingers were covered with a red blotch. It almost matched the one on her arm and she silently wondered when she'd gotten so freaking clumsy.

With her back to both men, she ran her hand under cool water, blotted it dry and then smeared a generous amount of burn ointment on it. At the rate she was going, they should take out stock in the stuff.

The scraping of chair legs startled her into turning around. Clay and Chance were both standing beside her.

"Damn, again?" Clay asked as Chance said, "Here, let me see that."

Bobbie could do nothing but relent. Two oversized men towering over her were too much for her to protest. Even worse was the fact that one was condescending as hell, while it seemed the other wanted to coddle and protect her.

"No. I'm fine. Would you both just sit and eat already before it gets cold?" Then she followed her own suggestion.

They'd just about finished the meal when Clay slowly lowered his fork to the table. Bobbie watched in horror as he moved his hand to his lips and none-too-subtly removed the piece of eggshell from his mouth, glaring at her as he did so. It was one of many times already this morning that Bobbie fervently wished the floor would open up and swallow her whole.

"I think I'll get started cleaning upstairs," she said as an excuse to get away from the table. "Don't worry about the dishes. I'll do them when I'm finished."

Bobbie's legs couldn't move fast enough to get her out of the room, but her knees were shaking so hard she had no choice but to slow down once she reached the living room.

"Dammit, Clay, did you have to be such a bastard?" she heard Chance say.

"That woman's a menace, Chance, and you damned well know it. I don't know what in the hell you were thinking when you hired her."

She didn't wait around to hear what Chance's answer was, and she sure as hell wasn't going to shed any tears over Clay's terse words. In fact, she felt more determined than ever. She'd show him that she could do what was expected of her. Yet at the same time, she sighed in relief when she remembered that the Bodine's long-term housekeeper was due back sometime in the afternoon.

With renewed determination and the motivation to prove herself to Clay, Bobbie straightened the upstairs rooms to the best of her ability. Several times she found herself at the window. The view was magnificent from the second-story window. The first time she'd taken a break to look, it was to see Chance mount a horse and head off through the pasture. Clay, who had been watching, disappeared into the barn after Chance left.

When she'd finished cleaning upstairs, Bobbie headed down to start on the kitchen. She'd just dried the last dish and was about to place it in the cupboard when a feisty voice startled her from the doorway. "Who are you and what are you doing in my kitchen?"

The plate slipped from Bobbie's hand and shattered on the floor. "If today gets any worse, I swear I'm going straight to bed and never coming out." Bobbie grumbled the words as she turned to return stares with an older, gray-haired woman.

"You must be Mildred. Chance has told me so much about you. Welcome home," Bobbie greeted as she knelt to pick up the broken plate, earning herself a nice cut in the process. To round out an already exasperating day, she proceeded to drip blood up the cabinet door and over the sink before ever making it to the faucet.

There was just something about the sight of her own blood that didn't settle well, so it took a minute of dizziness before her muddled mind thought to grab a towel in order to staunch the flow.

"Oh, my," Mildred exclaimed as she bustled forward.

"I'm fine, really." Bobbie was damned sure she'd muttered those very same words at least a dozen times since coming to the Lazy B. "It's not as bad as it looks."

"I'll be the judge of that, now let's have a look-see."

"You are Mildred, aren't you?" Bobbie asked in hopes of keeping her mind off of what the woman was doing.

"I am. And who might you be?"

"I'm Bobbie Carlington. Chance hired me to help out around here."

For a moment the woman just stared at her. "I heard Clay and Chance talking about bringing on a kid by the name of Bobbie but you certainly aren't a kid. I'd venture to say that Clay's had a thing or two to say since your arrival."

"More like three or four," she said, not at all trying to hide the sarcasm in her voice.

"So what have you been doing to help out?" Mildred's gaze was sharp. She narrowed her eyes just a bit, making Bobbie feel as if her answer made a huge difference.

"Not much. I made sandwiches for supper last night but that was only after I dropped the pan of lasagna on the floor. This morning I made scrambled eggs with shells in 'em, burnt toast and coffee so awful Clay wouldn't even drink it." Bobbie didn't realize her voice broke at the last and nearly missed when Mildred muttered a not-so-nice comment about Clay under her breath.

Doggedly, she went on. "I straightened things upstairs and had just finished the breakfast dishes when you came in."

"Sounds like you've been busy." Mildred shifted her gaze back to Bobbie's finger. "Looks like you might need a stitch or two."

Bobbie shook her head. "No, I'm sure it will be all right." There was no way in hell she was going to make the fuss of a hospital visit for a cut to her finger that further proved just how inept she was at keeping house.

Mildred checked the cut one more time before nodding. "Why don't you go on up to your room and rest for just a bit?" She was so sweet Bobbie couldn't help but take her up on the offer. She'd study instead of rest, but no one needed to know. What she did on her own time

was her business and it would be best if she kept it that
way.

Chapter Three

Mildred confronted Clay and Chance as soon as they stepped through the door. Hands balled on her ample hips, she was madder than a wet hen. "You boys have got some explaining to do." Her voice shook with anger.

"Not me. I didn't have a damned thing to do with it."

Chance squinted. It appeared as if he were silently pleading with Clay. He had to know Mildred wasn't about to let his boyish good looks sway her.

"Sorry, but you're the one who did it, so you can explain." Clay left the room, making a quick escape. Mildred, who was like a second mother to them, knew the last thing they wanted to do was hurt her feelings, but she wanted answers.

"Now just sit down a minute, Mildred, and let me explain."

"What's there to explain? Evidently you think I can't do my job but I don't understand what gave you that idea. Hell, boy, I could work circles around you." Mildred finally took a seat at the table.

Chance poured a cup of coffee for Mildred and then sat beside her. "It's not what you think."

Mildred turned, giving him her full attention. "Remember when I went to that horse auction in Oklahoma?"

At her nod, Chance continued. "While I was there, I met Bobbie. She was working for the stable where I bought Lady. She was Lady's owner and she wasn't only losing her horse, but her job. We talked for a while and went out a few times and that was all it took before I knew she would be perfect."

Mildred's wide-eyed stare must have confused him. She knew her cheeks were red, she could feel the heat. Her chest puffed up, her indignation was so great. She stood in one swift motion, thrust a single finger in Chance's face and shook it for all it was worth.

"You listen and you listen good. I only spent a few minutes with that young lady, so can't say I know her, but that don't matter no how. What I do know is that I won't let you take advantage of her. I'm ashamed of you, Chance Bodine. You were raised better than that!"

Chance was laughing before she could finish her tirade. "Please sit down, Mildred. I didn't mean I wanted her for myself. I think she's perfect for Clay."

That got Mildred quiet real quick. "You think that's wise? It's obvious from just lookin' at her that the girl is quite young."

"I know." Chance sighed. "And I'll admit to having some doubts myself, now that she's here. Clay doesn't seem to care much for her. He's been nothing but rude and obnoxious since she got here."

Mildred scowled. "So I heard. You can bet your sweet bippy he won't be treatin' her wrong while I'm around. I'll pinch his head off if he does."

Mildred could tell Chance was having the damndest time not laughing. He had trouble hiding his grin when she turned and gave him a determined look. "Well, boy, what's the plan?"

"Don't really have one. Just thought I'd throw them together as much as possible and see what happens."

"All right, I'll help as much as I can. Might have to send her out some to help outside and of course, she could help Clay with some of the office business," Mildred said, thinking aloud. "It's probably a good idea to keep her out of the kitchen. She told me she'd had a few problems before I got here and the first thing I saw when I walked through the door was the poor thing on the verge of fainting from the blood."

"Blood?"

"Yeah, I startled her into dropping a plate and she cut herself picking up the mess. Might want to check it out, she was a bit squeamish and I didn't get a good look. I think she might need a stitch or two."

"Damn," Chance swore as he left the kitchen.

ॐ

Clay was sitting in the living room reading the newspaper when Chance came stomping in from the kitchen. "What's the matter now?"

"Mildred said Bobbie cut her finger and was bleeding all over when she got home this afternoon. She thinks I ought to go take a look and that it may need a stitch or two."

Clay just shook his head. Bobbie Carlington was a distraction of the worst kind. If she wasn't breaking things and ruining his dinner, she was setting his body on fire.

"Go check on her then." He knew if he were the one to go, he wouldn't be able to keep his hands off her luscious body. He didn't know what to think about her or what to do with her. Sure, he could think of a few things to do to her. Her large, full breasts would beckon him and he didn't know if he'd be able to ignore the call. It was the after effects he worried about.

From her reaction to seeing him nude last night, Clay was sure she was fairly innocent, and the last thing he needed was a clingy woman, especially one who lived under the same roof. Once again, he mentally lectured himself to leave Bobbie alone.

Chance grumbled something about being an idiot before he headed up the stairs to check on Bobbie. For several minutes Clay was overwhelmed by jealousy. It was silly since he'd been the one to insist Chance go, and yet he wanted to be the one to tend to her wounds. If the past day showed any type of pattern, she was prone to accidents, which meant he would constantly be tending to her. The more the thought ran through his mind, the less it disturbed him. It was as if he'd suddenly become okay with the thought of taking care of Bobbie, accident prone or not.

When several minutes passed by with no word from upstairs, Clay began to pace. Maybe she really was hurt.

"Damn, I should have gone instead of sending my knucklehead brother," he muttered under his breath. He'd just reached the bottom of the staircase when he spotted Chance coming down.

"She all right?"

"She could have used a couple of stitches, but she refused to go to the hospital so I used some of that skin mending glue. It'll do."

"What in the hell do you mean she refused to go? If she needs medical attention, she'll go whether she wants to or not." He couldn't believe his ears. She was a grown woman, not a child.

Clay's foot had just landed on the first step when Chance grabbed his arm. "Leave her be." Chance's tone was determined. "You've done and said enough to her already."

"And that matters to you because?" Clay knew he was being an ass but Chance's protectiveness toward Bobbie rubbed him the wrong way. "Is there more going on, Chance? I thought you said she just needed a job."

Chance's eyes narrowed. His cheeks colored at Clay's insinuation but Clay wasn't ready to back down just yet.

He had to know where Chance stood. Was he attracted to Bobbie in more than just a friendly way?

"If you just wanted to bring her home, you could have set her up in one of the empty cabins."

"Don't," Chance growled. "Bobbie's a good girl and I'll knock your ass out before I let you say another bad word about her."

Clay knew he was wrong and the last thing he wanted to do was drive a wedge between him and his brother. Even through the jealousy, Clay knew he'd been an ass to Chance. It was only right to apologize.

"Dammit, I know. I'm sorry, Chance. Shit, man, she's driving me fucking crazy." Clay spoke only the truth. He just hoped his brother hadn't picked up on exactly how Bobbie was getting to him. It was amazing how deep she'd burrowed beneath his thick skin in such a short amount of time. Just looking at her made him hard, and that made him angry. He'd always been able to keep his body under control, but there was something about Bobbie that drew him like a moth to a flame, and he was powerless to fight it.

It would do no good for Chance to know that every time she so much as stepped into a room, his cock grew rigid with anticipation. Or how he longed to dominate her, to demand she submit to his every whim. Nope, with the mood Chance was in right now, that would probably only earn him a black eye or two.

Chance seemed to have relaxed a bit. "Just give her some time, Clay, and stop riding her so hard."

Clay almost snorted at that. If he was riding her hard, he wouldn't be feeling as frustrated as he was. "So, her finger really is okay?"

"Yeah, it's fine. I'm not sure if it's needles she's afraid of or the doctor in general, but she kicked up a fuss when I mentioned it. Instead of upsetting her, I just let it be. I'm sure it's fine."

Chance was almost out of the room when he turned back. "By the way, I agreed to take Bobbie into town tomorrow. She wants to find a used car."

ಜಿ

Bobbie woke extra early the next morning. She dressed quickly, then darted down the stairs as quietly as possible so as not to wake anybody up. She'd forgotten how early ranching started though, because upon arriving at the kitchen, Mildred was already busy preparing breakfast.

"Mornin'."

"Morning, missy. Now why don't you sit down there and I'll serve you up some biscuits and gravy. Looks like you could use a good breakfast."

Bobbie looked down at her size twelve denim-clad thighs and wondered if Mildred had somehow missed them, or the load she was carrying on her chest.

"No thanks." She reached into the refrigerator for a diet soda instead. She popped open the can and took a sip before grabbing a snack cake out of the cabinet. "I've got some stuff I have to do before Chance takes me into town this morning, so I'll just take these with me. Thanks anyway." She scurried from the kitchen, afraid she wouldn't get back to her room before Clay showed up.

Bobbie wasn't at all sure why she was keeping her correspondence courses a secret, but she was. It was hard work, but by the time she finished her courses, she'd be able to get a bookkeeping job somewhere. She wouldn't be beholden to someone else for a roof over her head or the junk food in her belly.

When a soft knock sounded at her door, Bobbie shuffled her papers until they were neatly stacked and put them in the desk drawer. "Just a minute," she mumbled and grabbed her bag off the chair.

When she opened the door, Chance looked over her shoulder as if she were hiding something. It made her feel a bit guilty for not having told him about her educational pursuits.

"You ready?" she asked, trying to deflect the questions she saw in his eyes.

"Sure am. Thought we should head out early so we can get back early."

"Sounds good to me."

A few minutes later they were bouncing along in his truck. A friendly, companionable silence lingered around them, but not for long.

"Heard you stormed the kitchen for junk again this morning. Should probably warn you that my brother won't let you get away with that often."

"Well I don't really see where it's any of Clay's business what I eat." The thought of someone telling her what she could and couldn't eat was crazy. It was simple as far as Bobbie was concerned. Junk food tasted better than the healthy stuff, so why not eat it if that was what she wanted?

Chance gave her a dazzling smile. "For the most part, I agree with you, but Clay doesn't see it that way. He sees that you're living at the Lazy B, therefore you are under his care. It's clear cut in his eyes."

"I'm fine, Chance, and I'm too old to have someone telling me what to eat. Besides, it's okay because I even it out with healthy food every now and then."

"I can see why you'd think that. Me, now, I'm wondering when you sleep."

When her jaw dropped and stayed there, he gave a low chuckle. "I'm not spying, Bobbie. It's just that I heard you up for most of the night. Clay could sleep through a world war, but not me."

Bobbie really wanted to explain why she stayed up late at night but she didn't. After the mess she'd made of things yesterday, she was pretty sure he wouldn't believe her if she told him she was taking accounting classes and was actually good at it.

Nope, for now she would just keep her secret to herself.

"I think I'm going to need more time to get used to being in a new place, not to mention the time difference."

He seemed to take her word for it and changed the subject. "So what type of car are you looking for?"

"Nothing fancy," she said with a mischievous twinkle in her eye. "Anything fast will do." Chance laughed, shook his head at her, and concentrated on the road. Once again they sat side by side in silence, but it wasn't overwhelming. It was comfortable.

ొ

It only took an hour to talk the salesman down to a price she could afford. At first, Bobbie was reluctant to give the money up. Chance figured Bobbie's reluctance stemmed from the fact that deep inside, she'd hoped to buy Lady back.

"I already told you she's there anytime you want to ride her. Anytime at all, okay?" He gently nudged her chin up with his finger.

"I know and I thank you." She turned to the used car salesman. "I'll take it." Bobbie smiled, handing him the cash.

An hour later the paperwork was completed, and she and Chance were off to lunch.

"Let's celebrate," she said, hopping into her new used car as Chance climbed into his truck.

At the diner, they talked over greasy burgers and even greasier fries. When they were done, Chance insisted on paying the tab, not giving an inch when Bobbie suggested they split it.

"If you'd like, you can follow me over to the bank. After, I'll follow you on home. My business there doesn't usually take that long."

"I'll be all right. I need to stop and stock up on some junk food and then I'll head on out. See you later this evening." Bobbie waved as she lowered herself into the little red sports car.

At the grocery store, she stocked up on munchies and what others would consider a month's supply of soda. Only Bobbie would be lucky if the two cases lasted her a week.

Bobbie took the ride through town slow, taking notice of everything around her. She noticed what appeared to be the local hangout. It was still early afternoon but there were already a few cars parked in front. A sign hanging over the front door deemed the place the Electric Cowboy. It sounded like fun so Bobbie promised herself that right after payday, she'd go out and have some fun.

Chapter Four

Clay began the short trek from the stable to the house, his mind cluttered with thought. The day had been long and hard without Bobbie. He'd worked his fingers to the bone repairing a section of downed fence trying to keep her off his mind. He hadn't liked it at all. It was amazing how she could light up a room with just her smile. It was doubly amazing how quickly she'd reeled him in without even trying.

The last thing in the world he wanted was to develop feelings for her, but it seemed that was exactly what he was doing. Clay was yanked back from his wandering thoughts when he noticed a cloud of dust on the road leading to the ranch. A sure sign of trouble was heading his way.

His first thought was for the safety of his ranch hands. He did some mental calculating trying to remember where everyone was working for the day, tense with anticipation for the possible emergency.

When a wind-up toy of a sports car skidded to a halt in front of the house, Clay relaxed briefly, realizing it wasn't an emergency. He was glad it wasn't one of the ranch trucks, but he'd be having a few words with whoever was in the car that thought it was okay to drive like a bat out of hell.

"Damned crazy-ass drivers," he spat.

Clay's long legs ate up the ground quickly as he strode with purpose to the little red car. He halted in his tracks the minute the door was thrust open. The cherub face and wide green eyes behind the wheel were all too familiar.

Bobbie climbed from the low-slung car as if she didn't have a care in the world and it made Clay see red. If she drove like that on a country road, he was afraid to think of the speed she'd accomplished on the highway between town and the Lazy B.

When Bobbie finally spotted him, she stopped what she was doing and held one hand up to her face to block out the sun. She was smiling and squinting against the sun as if she were trying to see him better. Clay did nothing to remove the irate look from his face.

Her smile faltered, replaced by a look of worry. His anger burning, Clay didn't even think to smile when she turned to look over her shoulder as if searching for the poor fool who had the audacity to anger the boss man to the point of eruption.

When she spotted no one, she quickly turned back around, but it was too late for escape, he was already at her side. He took a deep breath, trying to rein in his temper. It seemed he'd been taking a lot of deep breaths in the short time since Bobbie had been at the Lazy B.

"That sorry excuse for a car can't be safe going the speed limit, much less flying down country roads," he yelled, his anger once again teetering on edge. Clay stared at her. It was a look he'd used before to ward off even the biggest of men and couldn't help but be surprised when Bobbie didn't seem to notice.

She simply raised a delicately arched brow and acted as if he hadn't said a word. When she turned her back to him and reached into what there was of a backseat, he lost it. Clay firmly grasped Bobbie's wrist and spun her back until she faced him. Her bones felt small and fragile beneath his large hand so he relaxed his hold accordingly, but refused to release her when she protested his treatment.

Her green, glittering cat eyes widened briefly before they narrowed on him.

"Just what in the hell do you think you're doing?"

"Me? What do you mean what am I doing!" she demanded right back. "I can't believe you have the audacity to lay your hands on me and then ask me what I'm doing."

Her cheeks were flushed, her eyes icy and intense. He wasn't sure if she'd ever looked more beautiful than she did just then. Her body shook. With what emotion, he couldn't be sure.

Clay loosened his grip on her wrist slightly but didn't step away. "Only fools with a death wish drive like that, dammit!"

The thought of her mangled body lying in the twisted wreckage of the tiny red sports car haunted his vision. Just thinking of it made his tightly leashed fury break loose, especially when she continued to act the victim.

"Let me go, you big ass!" Bobbie struggled to free her wrist from his grasp.

The more she tried to wriggle free, the tighter he held her. Before she could say another word, Clay clamped an arm around her waist and drew her curvy body tightly to him.

Her large breasts branded him, just as her lower belly brushed his now throbbing cock. Her every movement caused him untold sexual agony. He wanted nothing more than to throw her to the dirt and bury his cock deep within her.

"Stay still, dammit!" he commanded when her struggles had him teetering on the edge.

"Get your damned hands off me." Bobbie renewed her effort to get free.

"I'll put my hands on you all right, you little fool. If I catch you driving like that again, it'll be my hand on your backside that you'll feel."

Clay's mouth crushed hers. There was nothing sensual about it. His action demanded her surrender. Bobbie's body stiffened as he continued to hold her tight. When he forced his tongue into the sweet haven of her mouth, she moaned. The sound was rough and low, as if she'd fought to stop it. That thought brought Clay up short. His body ached for more. More than he was ready to deal with just yet.

Clay thrust Bobbie from him, causing her to falter briefly before regaining her balance.

It was then that Clay noticed the ghostly pallor of her face. Her eyes glittered as she looked around wildly. Several of the men had made it back. It seemed all were raptly watching them, including Mildred, who looked on from the screened front door.

Bobbie opened her mouth to speak but quickly closed it. Her color was back, only now it rode high on her cheeks. With her head high, she skirted around him and walked quickly toward the house, not saying a word to anyone along the way.

"Son of a bitch!" He couldn't believe the way he'd treated her. How easy he lost his temper around her. How easy he lost control. How easy it was to care for her. It was the latter that had him worried. Bobbie Carlington didn't seem too inclined to have a man around, most importantly, not one as demanding as he was.

"She's getting to you," Mildred said as she approached Bobbie's car where he still stood. It wasn't a question, so Clay didn't give an answer. Instead, he muttered something about nosy females as he grabbed Bobbie's bags from the back of her car and made his way past a grinning Mildred into the house.

Supper that night was a quiet occasion. Bobbie chased the food around her plate but ate very little. She kept out of the conversation and refused to make eye contact with any of them. Chance and Mildred both glared at Clay as if her sullen mood was his fault. As soon as the meal was finished, he closed himself in the study. He was so far behind in paperwork he wasn't sure he'd ever get caught up. Bookkeeping was his least favorite thing to do as far as ranch business went, which was why he usually waited until the last possible moment before taking care of it. The top of his desk was lost beneath a mountain of papers and he was out of patience. With himself, Bobbie, and the whole damned situation.

ଚ

After supper, Bobbie offered to wash the dishes but was quickly shooed out of the kitchen. Mildred claimed it was due to her finger, but Bobbie knew better. Since being hired on, she'd done nothing but bungle every attempt she made to help.

She was still extremely embarrassed by what had happened between her and Clay earlier that afternoon. What was even more mortifying was the fact that her traitorous body remembered every second his arms had held her, the way his mouth possessed hers.

Even now, her nipples were peaked and her panties wet. It was very disturbing to think she could get turned on by someone manhandling her and remain that way. There had been a few minutes during their confrontation when Bobbie had actually feared for her safety. It hadn't lasted long, but it was enough to warn her off Clay for good.

She didn't need a man and wanted one even less. Her father had proved early on that men were nothing but trouble. He'd claimed to love her mother even as he ignored her unless it was to his benefit to pay attention to her.

The thought of her mother brought a mist of tears to Bobbie's eyes. God hadn't created a better woman than Minnie Carlington. She'd been gentle and patient and had given Bobbie enough love to compensate for what her father held back.

It was days like today when Bobbie realized most what she'd lost that fateful night four long years ago. It had been heart wrenching to wake up in the hospital with no more than a mild concussion, and learn that neither of her parents had made it out alive. Barely seventeen, Bobbie hadn't been sure if she'd wanted to survive.

It took time and a lot of help from Mac McQuinn, but eventually Bobbie started to live again. Not only did she start to live, she did it in a new way. She tried to live every day as if she were dying, as if it would be her last.

Even as she physically moved forward, she'd not been able to mentally and emotionally connect herself with others. She'd tried to keep her life simple so she wouldn't have to deal with the pain of losing another loved one and so far it had worked. Except for Mac, and now those at the Lazy B, Bobbie lived a solitary life.

As much as Bobbie tried to fight it, she knew her time of lonely living was over. She'd made friends over the past few days and it felt good. It was something she hoped to expand on. It felt good to care. Even though she was willing to let her guard down a bit, she wasn't sure how she felt about allowing Clay into that equation. She had a sneaking suspicion he'd walk all over her if she let him. When it came to matters of the heart, it was hard to keep things simple, she thought as she walked out the front door and onto the porch.

The night air was crisp. Its freshness filled her lungs as she inhaled deeply.

"Hey, Bobbie," a voice called from the dark, causing her to jump. "Sorry," the voice said.

Bobbie could barely make out the figure of a man, but she wasn't afraid. As the man moved closer to the light, Bobbie thought she recognized him. "Rick?" she asked hesitantly, not sure if that was his name or not. She'd only met him once before, on her first day at the ranch. Rick worked for Clay and Chance and from what she'd heard so far, he was a hard-working man whom the Bodines trusted wholeheartedly.

"Yeah, it's me." He answered her from the bottom step. "I thought I'd come by and invite you out with a group of us who'll be going in to town after payday for a bit of fun. You game?"

Bobbie thought about it for a second before answering. "Sure. Why not?" It sounded like fun to her.

"I'll pick you up about six," Rick offered, a friendly smile on his face.

"Thanks anyway, but I'd rather meet you all there."

"Sounds good. See you then." Rick gave Bobbie a quick wave as he disappeared into the dark.

Bobbie moved to the bench swing and sat on its cushioned surface with a sigh. The gentle rocking motion combined with the rose-scented breeze relaxed her more than she thought possible and she drifted to sleep.

A flutter at her cheek woke her up. It was Clay. He was standing in front of her, his fingers alternately stroking her cheek and playing with her hair. He seemed to be deep in thought. His gaze was lowered, his free hand shoved deep into his pocket. It was an eerie feeling to be so close to him, to be able to study him without his knowledge. It somehow seemed wrong.

Bobbie moved, drawing his attention to her. "No, don't go." His voice was low. Her heart fluttered uncontrollably. "I won't hurt you, darlin'. I promise."

"I know," she heard herself say. Bobbie wasn't sure where the words had come from after the day she'd had, but she knew they were true.

He gave her a crooked smile as if he'd read her mind. "You mind?" Clay motioned to the vacant spot next to her.

She shook her head and began to scoot over. "Uh uh, stay where you are." He placed a large palm high on her thigh to make sure she didn't budge. Then he lowered his six-foot frame into the spot next to her. They were so close Bobbie could feel the heat radiate off of him in waves, engulfing her in warmth. One of his fingers made tiny little circles on her thigh. She watched it, fascinated and worried at the same time. He was going to drive her crazy if he didn't stop.

"I've tried not to, sweetheart," Clay whispered as his mouth moved toward hers. "I've done everything in my power not to want you but it's a losing battle. One I'm no longer willing to fight."

With the tip of a finger, Clay turned Bobbie's head until she faced him. The last of his sentence was breathed against her mouth just before her lips were crushed against his. His teeth nipped and nibbled, his tongue plundered and Bobbie could do nothing about it.

She felt her body melt into his, felt the heat all the way through to her center and agonized over what to do about it. When his mouth wandered lower, grazing the uppermost swell of her breast, all thought fled her mind. She was left with nothing but an all-consuming need to feel, to experience everything he was doing to her.

By the time he tore his mouth from her flesh, they were both panting. "Come up here." Clay helped her straddle his thighs. The position was a bit awkward but Bobbie didn't mind. She was willing to do anything to get her body closer to Clay's.

Clay took advantage of Bobbie's position by lifting her shirt until the hem rested at the top of her large breasts.

"Oh, darlin', I knew you'd be beautiful but this was more than even I imagined." His voice was husky. It rubbed every nerve ending, making her pussy flood. Bobbie tunneled the fingers of both hands through his hair pulling him closer. She wanted his mouth on her, sucking her nipples until she screamed for him to stop. It surprised her how much she wanted something she'd never experienced before.

"Please, Clay." When he pulled at the edge of her bra cup with his teeth, Bobbie groaned.

"Please what, baby? Tell me what you want."

She could feel the weight of her breasts as he unhooked the front clasp of her bra. The cool breeze caused her nipples to harden even further.

"I want your mouth on me." The words embarrassed her, but they also made her hot. Clay insisting she tell him what she wanted aroused her even more. The fact that Clay could so easily send her body spiraling out of control distressed Bobbie. She did all she could to push such thoughts from her mind. That was something she'd give thought to later, she promised herself.

She bit her lip in an effort to keep her lusty moans silent. It shocked her to realize how much she wanted to cry out in ecstasy as his mouth closed over her full nipple, sucking it deep into his mouth. She wanted to chant his name and scream as her orgasm neared and spilled over, causing her inner muscles to spasm in wave after wave of blissful release, but she didn't dare.

"Mmm." Clay hummed against her other nipple. "Sweet, just like honey."

She felt his hands shift, his fingers plucked at the fastening of her jeans. It was tricky but he eventually got them undone and before she had time to prepare for the erotic assault, he was stroking her clit.

"Oh God," she gasped as he played her body. She could do little to control herself as her hips rocked back and forth.

As he drew deeply from her breast again, tugging and nipping at her nipple, Bobbie climaxed. It was overwhelming in its intensity and seemed to last forever. Clay's fingers continued to tease and torture, as did his mouth, until her body was sated and limp lying against him.

She was dozing lightly, her body completely satisfied, when Mildred's voice awoke her and sent her scurrying from Clay's lap. Her cheeks flamed as she struggled to right her clothes.

"Bobbie. You still out here?" Mildred repeated.

"Yes, Mildred. I'm still out here." She hollered back, praying the woman didn't come outside.

Bobbie tried hard to hide her dismay when the screen door squeaked open and Mildred stepped out onto the porch. Clay just sat there, a smug look on his face. He was obviously aroused, if the bulge at the front of his jeans was any indication, but he did nothing to cover himself.

Bobbie watched with dread as Mildred looked from her to Clay and back. "Sorry to interrupt. I thought you were alone. I just wanted to say good night."

"Thanks." Bobbie tried in vain to keep her composure. Clay was still smiling like an idiot and for some reason it made Bobbie angry. "I was just heading that way myself."

She briefly enjoyed the fact that her words wiped the smile from Clay's lips.

Mildred nodded to the both of them, mumbled good night and retreated into the house.

"What in the hell is wrong with you?" Bobbie hissed. "Couldn't you even cover yourself?" She waved in the general direction of his lap.

Clay chuckled. "She knows you belong to me now just the same as if I'd said the words, so there's no need to hide anything."

His words hit Bobbie like a ton of bricks. "I don't belong to anyone." Bobbie backed away from him.

"Whatever you say, baby. Go on up to your room. We'll talk about this tomorrow."

She shook her head, then couldn't seem to stop the negative movement. "No. No we won't," she answered before she headed in the house. Bobbie didn't slow down until she was safely behind her bedroom door and it was locked tight.

Bobbie blindly removed her clothes for a shower. A cold shower, she amended. It wasn't until she was facing the mirror that she saw it. A hickey, so dark it was almost purple, marred her pale skin just above where her neck and shoulder met. Bobbie wasn't sure whether to scream or spit she was so mad. "The damned asshole is gonna suffer for this." She headed for the shower, cursing the whole way.

Chapter Five

Clay couldn't get Bobbie out of his mind. Her taste, the way she'd moved against his hand, riding his fingers with wild abandon until she'd climaxed so beautifully he thought he would come without so much as a touch.

He remembered how her luscious body had melted against him and he couldn't forget how wonderful she had felt. That had been four days ago. Four torturously long days ago and Clay wasn't sure how much longer he was going to be able to handle not touching or tasting her.

The red-haired vixen was driving him insane. She hadn't said more than ten words to him in that time and the words she had said had been yelled at the top of her lungs.

Clay could still picture the way Bobbie had looked when she'd come down the stairs, her red hair flowing wildly around her shoulders. Clay's groin tightened at the sight of her, at the remembered taste of her nipples against his lips. It was her eyes that had intrigued him most on that bright and sunny morning, though. Flashing green and narrowed at him in anger, they were absolutely magnificent.

"I don't know what in the hell you thought you were doing," she'd hollered. "I'm not some fucking cow you can brand, you know." She pulled her hair away from her neck so he could see the hickey he'd left.

He couldn't help the smile that crossed his mouth. He'd taken great pleasure in marking her. He wanted everyone to know she was taken. He might be considered old fashioned, but he figured he'd laid claim to her and the sooner everybody realized it, the better off they'd be because he wouldn't have anyone else trying to stake a claim on what he considered his.

"What I know is that you'd better watch your mouth, darlin'. That's no way for a lady to be talking."

"Oh, go screw yourself, cowboy. I've never pretended to be a lady and sure as hell don't look like one with this damned thing on my neck." She must be pissed, Clay thought. He'd never heard her use foul language.

"I won't warn you again, Bobbie. If you can't curb your tongue I'm sure I can find something for it to do."

The look on her face had been comical until he'd added, "I told you everyone would know you belong to me. There's no mistaking it now so you might as well get used to it."

Without further words or action, Bobbie had turned and left the room and hadn't looked his way since. Clay meant to remedy that problem today if he had to track her down and drag her back kicking and screaming. Since Bobbie was spending most of her time outside or closed up in her room in order to avoid him, Clay knew he'd have to go in search of her.

It was almost an hour later when Clay walked into the dimly lit interior of the stables. The pleasantly familiar scent of hay, leather and horse wafted around him, assaulting his senses.

A horse neighed behind its stall door. It was then that Clay heard it, Bobbie's soft, crooning voice. She'd been spending a lot of time in the barn since their confrontation. He peered into the nearest stall and immediately noticed it had been cleaned. The stall's occupant nuzzled his hand while munching on something.

Walking the length of the long building, Clay checked each stall only to find the same results. He then knew Bobbie had meant what she'd said.

"I intend to work for my keep." Her words rolled around in his head. At the time, though, he'd given them little thought.

Clay was curious to see how Bobbie interacted with the mare when she thought she was alone, so he headed to the stall Lady now called home. For a few minutes, he just stood and watched as she stroked Lady's coat until it gleamed. She took special care with the animal, talking low, her voice soothing. She was gentle and patient as she worked every inch of Lady's coat.

Her actions made Clay jealous. He knew damned well it was crazy to be jealous of a horse. He couldn't help the way he felt though, the way his body reacted as he watched her hands stroke Lady. His cock throbbed behind the button fly of his jeans in hopes of being stroked the exact same way. Shifting position helped ease the ache only slightly. He feared nothing, or no one save Bobbie, would ease the ache permanently.

He didn't make a sound and yet she stilled as if she had some type of internal radar letting her know he was close by. Only this time he wasn't going to let her use it to get away from him. This time he meant business, and she was going to at least listen until he was done saying what he had to say.

Her head swiveled toward him, her eyes wide and wary. "What do you want, Clay?" Exasperation was evident in her voice.

"We need to talk. Come on out of there," he coaxed when she made no move to put away Lady's grooming supplies. The woman was mule-headed enough to test a saint and there wasn't much saintly about him.

ॐ

Bobbie sighed as she left Lady's stall. She'd put up a good fight, but it was over. Her body yearned for his touch. She turned into putty in his hands, which was the reason she'd stayed away. It had been a long, rough four days and Bobbie was tired of fighting.

The biggest battle had been the one she waged against her own body. Just the thought of him made her pussy weep. It was frustrating not being able to do anything to get rid of the ache deep inside of her.

She followed, her mind whirling, her body on fire, as Clay led them from Lady's stall to the back of the long building and into the makeshift office. It was a small room located right next to the tack room. Sparsely furnished, it held only a desk that sat in the center of the room with a chair on either side. The top of the desk was bare of personal items, but many pictures cluttered the walls. Some were of the horses, but many were of Clay and Chance as children.

The thought of being alone with Clay in such a secluded spot sent a shiver up Bobbie's spine. Whether from fear of the unknown, anticipation of what was to come, or a combination of them both, she wasn't sure.

The door closed behind her, but it was the soft click of the lock being engaged that caused her to flinch. Bobbie knew deep down inside what was going to happen and knew it was useless to try to stop it. She didn't want to stop it. Her body longed to be possessed by Clay, even as her independent spirit told her to run as fast as she could. Instead, she sat in one of the empty chairs and shook her head in amazement at his cockiness.

Clay was an arrogant ass, but a beautiful specimen of man, Bobbie thought, as she looked up at him. His thighs were strong, his hips narrow beneath the faded denim of his jeans. The wide expanse of Clay's chest looked wonderful with his usual cotton snap-up cowboy shirt stretched taut over it. His wavy brown hair was almost always covered by a wide brimmed cowboy hat, but what

Bobbie could see made her fingers itch to be buried deep within its thick strands.

He knelt directly in front of her and without a word, took her face in his hands and kissed her deeply. No prelude, no warm up. Just like that, and Bobbie was on fire for him.

His tongue traced her lips. Warm and wet, his mouth felt like heaven. She couldn't help the moan that escaped when his hand found her breast. He stroked and pleasured her, pulling her closer to the edge until she was writhing beneath his touch, pleading for more. When her breathing became labored and her skin shimmered with perspiration, he lifted her to her feet.

"Time to get out of these, baby," he said as he unfastened her pants. The feel of his work-roughened fingers against the skin of her abdomen sent a thrill of delight through her, causing her pussy to dampen her panties.

After slowly unbuttoning her pants, he lowered her zipper inch by agonizing inch, revealing the pale flesh of her abdomen. He toyed with the waistband of her lacy panties before slipping his hand beneath, allowing his fingers to glide through the tight curls covering her aching center before sliding her panties over her hips, letting them drop to the floor. He was keeping her off guard, on edge, and it was driving her crazy in the best possible way.

"I want these completely bare." He lifted her shirt over her head, leaving it to bind her arms briefly. The breath whooshed out of her lungs at the thought of being fucked by Clay while bound. He must have recognized the origin of her excitement.

"Like that, do you?" His voice was a low murmur.

Bobbie couldn't answer. Her cheeks flamed at the thought of telling him exactly what had been going through her mind.

"Answer me, Bobbie." His voice was still low but edged with steel. He was in command and wanted her to know it.

"No," Bobbie lied, too embarrassed to admit how much the thought of being tied down while he repeatedly buried himself in her slick pussy excited her. She should be horrified, not aroused.

Clay removed her bra completely, baring her to his gaze. He lowered his head and took an elongated nipple into his mouth, sucking it deep and hard. Her body tensed at the new sensation. It was almost too close to pain for her comfort, but God it felt wonderful, as the pleasure flowed straight from her taut nipple to her engorged clit. The pleasure was so intense, Bobbie almost came as a result.

"Tell me," he insisted.

"What?" She couldn't remember what the question had been. Her body was on fire.

"Tell me you want me to bind you, Bobbie. Tell me exactly how you want me to fuck that sweet pussy of yours."

"I...I can't." She just wanted him to fuck her already and yet, at the back of her mind, a niggling thought tried to break through her muzzy head. There was something she had meant to tell him but she couldn't concentrate when he was touching her. The thought was completely forgotten with his next words.

"Maybe not this time, darlin', but next time, you'll tell me what I want to hear."

Clay lifted her until she was perched on the edge of the desk. He moved in close. She could feel the length of his still-clothed body as he stood between her splayed thighs. His hands were everywhere, touching and teasing until she couldn't catch her breath.

His teeth nipped, his tongue laved and when he lowered himself to his knees, she gave not a single word of protest. She wasn't sure she could have put enough words together to form a sentence even if she'd wanted to protest.

Clay placed tender kisses up the inside of her knee as his hands caressed between her thighs. When he penetrated her with his large fingers, she thought she would collapse. When his breath replaced his fingers, she tensed and struggled to scoot her bottom back on the desk, separating her drenched pussy from his awaiting mouth.

Clay frowned and looked up at her, startling her into closing her eyes.

"Look at me, baby. I want to be sure you understand what I'm telling you." His voice was soothing, yet hard. He meant business, whatever it was he wanted to talk about.

"You can't do that." Bobbie whispered the words, completely mortified to be in such an undignified position.

"I can and I will. I can't believe you've never had anybody taste this sweet pussy of yours." He chuckled when she blushed. Bobbie could feel the heat invade her cheeks as it moved up her face.

His eyes narrowed as he grasped her thighs and pulled her until she was once again seated at the very edge of the desk. He swung both of her legs over his shoulders and placed her hands on either side of her thighs, folding her knuckles around the edge of the desktop.

"Stay just like that, darlin'. Don't move an inch."

Bobbie opened her mouth to speak, but Clay made one long swipe with his tongue that cleared her mind of any argument. He licked and lapped at her folds until she was in ecstasy. Bobbie couldn't contain the ear-splitting scream that tore from her throat when she came. Her body tensed and shuddered as if the climax would go on forever, its intensity almost painful.

Bobbie came back to herself as Clay stood, towering over her as he unfastened the buttons of his fly. He wore nothing beneath, allowing the thick length of his erection to spring free.

He moved between her thighs and kissed her so savagely she thought he would devour her. Bobbie could taste her essence on his lips. It wasn't disgusting like she'd thought it would be, but it was different.

"I want to touch you."

"Not this time, baby. If you touch me now, I'll explode." His voice was husky, hurried, as he laid her back on the hard surface of the desk. The sound of it aroused her further. To think that she could bring a man to such frenzy was empowering.

"I'm afraid I can't wait much longer as it is, darlin'." Clay apologized as his fingers grazed her clit, gliding over her slick skin, teasing and petting until she was once again mindless with need.

The feel of his body pressed against hers was incredible, making her gasp with pleasure. He was big and warm, but as his hands lifted her hips, preparing her for his entry, Bobbie remembered what it was that she hadn't told him.

"Clay." Bobbie was nervous, but afraid he would stop if she just blurted out the fact that she was a virgin.

Instead of answering her, Clay kissed her hungrily as he plunged his cock deep within her tight vagina. He groaned when her body gripped him as it struggled to accommodate his size.

Bobbie hadn't been prepared for his swift invasion. The initial pinch of pain caused her to stiffen and gasp against his mouth. Even as the initial pain subsided she still couldn't relax. Her body was on fire with the need for him to move.

She could feel her muscles pulse around Clay's cock. Every inch of her was filled with him. The erotic pressure continued to build even though Clay had yet to move. His hands left her and for a moment she was afraid to open her eyes.

"Good God!" Clay said. Bobbie opened her eyes at that and could see he was trying to control his temper. "Why in the hell didn't you say something?"

"I...I didn't..." was all Bobbie got out before Clay moved slightly within her. "Oh," she gasped. The feel of him moving so deeply within her sent stars shooting behind her eyes.

"Dammit," he thundered and stilled again.

"No, Clay, please don't stop," she begged when he stopped moving. She wanted him to move...no, she needed him to move.

"Just hold still." Clay tensed as if to move away.

Bobbie twined her arms around his neck. "Stay in me, Clay. Oh God," she panted. "If you don't do something, I'm gonna die. I just know I will."

She felt his body relax at her words. The first tentative movement of his hips was like water to a thirsty man. She couldn't get enough. Clay was like a drug, addictive and strong. Her body began to open up, yielding to his throbbing flesh and before long she was meeting him thrust for thrust. Their bodies met with intense pleasure until they were swept over with a climax so strong it was almost painful.

As the last of the spasms subsided, Bobbie relaxed, snuggling closer to Clay. She could get used to these secret rendezvous as long as she kept her heart right were it belonged, safe behind the brick wall her father had helped build for it all those years ago. If she could accomplish that, she'd be just fine.

It wasn't until Clay pulled away from her that she realized he was still mostly dressed, while she was completely naked. She looked up to comment on the fact that he was still dressed but the anger in his eyes stopped her short.

"Of all the damned idiotic things you've done in the last few days, that has to take the cake!"

Bobbie opened her mouth to protest but didn't have a chance to say a word before he laid into her again. "I could have hurt you. Did you ever stop to think of that?"

He didn't seem to be in the mood to let her speak, so she chose to stay quiet. "If you weren't..." he said, motioning to her.

Bobbie looked down at her nakedness, wondering what in the hell he was raving about. "Why I ought to..." Once again, he didn't finish his sentence. He bent down to retrieve her clothes but he didn't bother to hand them directly to her. Instead, he threw them on the desk next to her.

"Get your ass dressed and get back to the house." The words were forced out between his clenched teeth. He turned away so fast she wondered if he was disgusted by her presence or possibly her lack of dress.

Hurt and angry, Bobbie dressed as quickly as possible, confused by his treatment of her. Had she imagined the heated look he'd given her after he'd removed her clothes? She felt ashamed and couldn't stop the tears streaming down her cheeks. With as much dignity as possible, she slipped her shirt over her head, forgoing her bra altogether, stuffing it into her pocket instead.

She wanted to die, but since it wasn't likely that the ground would open up and swallow her whole, she decided the next best option was to make a hasty retreat. She watched Clay pacing back and forth, cursing and muttering. Without a word, Bobbie unlocked the door and left the office where she'd lost her virginity, thinking it was a damned good thing she hadn't also lost her heart.

Chapter Six

Clay ended the phone call feeling a bit ashamed at the relief coursing through his mind. He had just gotten off the phone with the bank manager who needed to go over some records with either himself or Chance. Clay saw it as an easy out and decided to attend the meeting himself. He needed time to think and a bit of business travel on behalf of the ranch was the perfect thing. He couldn't get Bobbie's face out of his mind. The way her body had moved beneath him haunted him every minute. The taste of her sweet nectar should be illegal, it was so wickedly good.

He'd had a feeling she was innocent, but a virgin? At her age? Clay shook his head, trying to clear the memory of how desolate Bobbie had looked when he'd run her out of the room. Ashamed at the way he'd treated her, Clay had headed back to the house only to find her bedroom door tightly closed.

Taking the easy way out, the coward's way, wasn't normal for Clay but that was exactly what he'd done. The thought disgusted him. Cursing himself for the fool he was, Clay headed for the coffee pot.

"I'm surprised Bobbie hasn't come down yet." Chance gave Clay a look that made him uncomfortable.

"It's still dark out, why would she?" countered Clay.

Clay poured himself a cup of coffee and sat across the table from Chance. "She usually comes down before now, grabs something quick and heads back up to her room."

Clay scowled. He'd never noticed Bobbie awoke so early and wondered why she did. She worked long, hard days, sometimes indoors but most often lately, she stayed in the stables and never complained. Now Clay wanted to know everything about her. She was a mystery and it bothered him that she'd never confided in him. Of course, he hadn't been the most hospitable person early on.

Clay decided the best defense against his nosy brother was to head out. He stood, grabbed his hat off the peg by the back door and turned to Chance. "I'll be back tonight or tomorrow morning at the very latest. Call if you need anything," he called over his shoulder to Chance, as he exited the door.

"Will do. You take care," Chance replied.

Guilt assaulted him as he all but fled the ranch before dawn. He would only be gone for the day, possibly overnight, but it would give him time to get things into perspective.

℞

It was only a three-hour drive, but his business meeting would last most of the afternoon, so Clay settled

69

into his seat, enjoying the drive while listening to soft country music. But not thirty minutes later, he figured he must be turning into a pussy-whipped man because this morning he couldn't wait to get away from the ranch, and now that he was gone, he couldn't wait to get home. Bobbie had gotten under his skin and even miles away, he couldn't stop thinking about her. "Go figure," he mumbled aloud to himself.

The afternoon passed quickly, his meeting went off without a hitch and before he knew it he was almost home. Throughout the day he'd replayed last night in his mind, trying to figure out how it impacted his future. And he kept coming to the same conclusion.

He needed to marry Bobbie Carlington. It was the proper thing to do. The thing Clay's old-fashioned values insisted upon.

Clay would pop the question as soon as he got back to the ranch. No sense in waiting, he thought, as he pulled off the highway and headed down the long gravel road leading home. Within minutes he could see the house on the horizon, and noticed Bobbie's car was parked in its usual spot. He'd just gotten out of the truck when Mildred rushed to the door. Her face was pinched with worry, hands clasped tightly in front of her.

Clay left his briefcase on the front seat and strode to the house as quickly as possible to see what was wrong.

"Everything all right?" he asked, knowing damned well it wasn't.

Mildred was shaking her head before he finished the question. "I was hoping you were Rick." She was a bit hesitant as she turned and headed toward the kitchen.

Clay followed, his temper rising right along with worry. "Why, Mildred? Tell me what's wrong."

"You'd better sit down, Clay." His heart skittered to a halt at her ominous words. He automatically thought something had happened to his parents. Or maybe it was his father's heart. After all, that was the reason his father had retired and left the running of the ranch to Clay. He readied himself for the blow to come.

"Bobbie's gone." Mildred's voice was barely above a whisper.

His mind didn't grasp her meaning. What did she mean gone, he'd seen her car parked right outside. "Gone where?" he asked impatiently.

"Um, well...I'm not sure. I found a note this morning saying she was going to go riding, but she hadn't returned by this afternoon. Chance rode out just a bit ago to look for her and Rick took the truck to check the boundary roads."

"She didn't say where she was going?"

Mildred shook her head as if she knew what was coming, and that words in Bobbie's defense would do no good.

"God dammit!" Clay roared. "What time?"

"Not too long after you left."

"And she hasn't been back to check in, in all that time?" Clay's mind whirled at the thought. His emotions reeled from one extreme to the next. When he got his hands on her, he was either going to throttle her or hug her tight and never let her go. And the whole time, he silently prayed she was okay.

"No, but I'm sure they'll be back real soon." Mildred's voice was cheery but it didn't show on her strained face.

&

Bobbie woke with a start, feeling the ground shake beneath her. For a hazy, sleep-befuddled moment, she thought the movement of the ground beneath her was an earthquake. She didn't actually know what an earthquake felt like, but she'd read about them and knew they were prevalent in California. This was different though. It was more like a rhythmic pounding that seemed to be getting closer.

It took Bobbie a minute to figure out what it was and when she finally did, she scrambled to her feet and made a beeline straight for Lady. From the position of the sun, Bobbie knew it was early evening and she was in deep shit.

Evidently her pity party had turned into an all day event and her nap had stretched to several hours. It had felt good to get away, to spend a day alone with no one to hound her, no work or studying. "I guess that's over," she mused wryly as the horse galloping toward her finally became clear in the distance.

The rider sat tall in the saddle, causing Bobbie's heart to pound furiously. She knew without a doubt that if the rider was Clay there was going to be hell to pay for her absence. Her hands shook with the knowledge of how angry he was going to be. While at the same time, it angered her to think he would act as if he cared when he obviously didn't.

His abrupt departure early that morning proved beyond a shadow of a doubt to Bobbie that Clay had gotten what he wanted from her. He obviously had no further use for a wild redhead with a plump figure. She'd already made up her mind that she wouldn't let his callous behavior get to her.

She only had one more lesson in her accounting course to complete, then she could schedule the final test. She'd been studying for the test for weeks and was confident she would pass. As soon as she did, she'd find a job in town and leave the Lazy B.

The thought made her frown just as it had earlier. She didn't want to leave the Lazy B because, despite the short amount of time she'd spent on the ranch, it had already begun to feel like home. It had since her very first day there. And working day in and day out with the folks on the ranch had made it feel even more so.

It was the first time she'd had friends or felt safe since her mother's death, not counting Mac, but if she stayed she'd be selling herself short. She didn't want a husband and she certainly had no plans to become the property of an arrogant cowboy. Even though the thought of leaving the Lazy B made her sad, she would have to do it or take the chance of being smothered by a man who didn't want anything more than to dominate her.

As the rider drew closer, Bobbie released an audible sigh of relief when she recognized Chance. He reined in the large Paint he was riding and dismounted in one fluid motion. He was at her side before she knew it.

"Are you okay?" he asked, looking her over from head to toe.

"I'm fine, Chance, and I'm sorry I'm so late. I needed time to think and I must have fallen asleep." She sheepishly motioned to the flattened grass under the copse of trees.

Chance chuckled and, with a conspiratorial wink, said, "Well, if we hurry we'll probably make it back to the ranch before Clay gets back."

Bobbie's sigh of relief that she might miss Clay's wrath had Chance laughing outright. She could only imagine what Clay would have done had it been him who had come looking for her instead of Chance.

When Chance finally got his laughter under control, he turned to Bobbie. "You sure everything is all right?"

"Yeah, I'm sure. I've just got a lot on my mind." When he kept watching her, she shook her head. "I'll explain another day, Chance. Right now I think we ought to head back."

Bobbie and Chance mounted their horses and headed back toward the house. They had just reached an area where the sprawling white ranch house was coming into view when they noticed him. The closer Clay's black stallion came, the further Bobbie's heart sank. He sat ramrod straight astride his horse. His commanding gaze was disturbingly intense and she knew she was in trouble. No amount of explaining would be enough for him.

Darting a pleading look to Chance, Bobbie reined Lady in and stopped. Not knowing what to do made her all the more nervous. She was well aware she had been wrong to go off alone, but she hadn't counted on falling asleep. At the time she left, Bobbie had only planned on being gone for an hour or so. Knowing that excuse would get her nowhere with Clay, she did the only thing she could think of; she stayed where she was and hoped for the best.

He was mad as hell, if the muscle twitching in his jaw was a clue, his determined face set in grim lines. There was no sign of the passionate man she had given her innocence to the day before. The man before her was unbending and set in his ways. She just hoped she would be able to talk herself out of whatever he had planned for her. Or at the very least, she hoped Chance would intervene and act as a buffer.

Bobbie watched in morbid fascination as Clay turned to Chance. "You can go back to the house now. I need to have a talk with Bobbie." His voice was astonishingly calm. That alone sent goose bumps skittering up Bobbie's spine. She wasn't sure if it was from fear or anticipation, but she was betting that soon fear would win hands down.

Bobbie, hoping to gain a bit of time to let Clay cool down, said, "That's okay, why don't we all go back together?" Her voice quivered. She cleared her throat and with a nonchalance she didn't feel, added, "That way I'll be able to get cleaned up. I'll explain everything at dinner."

With the words and a silent prayer on her lips, Bobbie turned Lady and started toward the house. But before she even went a couple of feet, Clay was by her side. Eyes flashing, he grabbed Lady's reins and gave a nod to Chance. Bobbie wanted to scream when Chance gave her an apologetic look before he left them alone.

Looking up, Bobbie noticed the fury in Clay's piercing brown eyes. For as long as she lived, she doubted she would ever forget the intensity of his stare. Yet, Bobbie couldn't seem to look away. The gold and amber flecks she saw in those flashing, angry eyes were burned into her memory.

With a firm grip on Lady's reins as well as his own mount's, Clay led them back to the group of trees where Bobbie had just taken her nap. Clay dismounted his horse, but before Bobbie had the chance to do the same, Clay did exactly what she'd expected him to do. He yanked her off Lady's back.

"Just what the hell did you think you were doing riding out alone?" he demanded. "Mildred is at the house worried sick about you. Do you know how irresponsible you've been? Not just irresponsible but stupid. It's just plain stupid to run off by yourself without letting anybody know where you're going or what time you'll be home."

The longer Clay ranted about her irresponsibility, the more not only her guilt grew, but her anger as well. She figured it was a defense mechanism on her part. Remembering how her father always belittled her mom for the smallest of things. Always telling her she could never do anything right. Bobbie could see her mother's dejected face in her mind and it gave her courage to stand up for herself and her actions.

She waited until he was done and then with her hands on her hips, Bobbie released all her own pent-up frustrations. "I don't need you telling me how to take care of myself, Clay. I've been doing it long enough and so far I've done just fine."

In a voice full of frustration, she added, "I am so tired of being talked to as if I were nothing more than a child you could punish that I could just scream!" She turned to walk away, "So you can go straight to hell, Clay Bodine."

Bobbie knew there was some perverse reason why she'd goaded him, knowing full well he was at the end of his rope. She figured that reason would come to her later, but she didn't want to think about it right now. All she wanted to do was leave with her dignity intact.

Before the idea that she had made a terrible mistake even had the chance to register fully, Clay seized her by the waist and swung her around. Their mutual anger vibrated between them as they stood, bodies pressed together intimately.

Nostrils flaring, Clay looked as if he was ready to pounce. He didn't give her the chance to speak, much less get away, before he carried her to a fallen log and sat, putting her over his knees.

"You keep acting like a naughty little girl and I'll treat you just like a naughty little girl." His voice was calm, tight with anger.

Before Bobbie had time to think or protest her position, Clay delivered a stinging blow to her bottom. For a second she was grateful for the cover of her jeans but soon realized the fabric, stretched tightly over her backside, was little help. It felt as if his hand was landing repeatedly on her bare skin.

"Damn, Clay, stop it already." Bobbie groaned when a stinging swat heated her upper thigh. She tried to ignore the way her clit rubbed against the seam of her pants as each blow thrust her against his hard thigh.

"Never again, Bobbie." Clay's hand landed again. "Tell me you'll never worry me like this again."

The sound of his voice caused her a moment of pause. Was that concern she'd heard? Was it possible he had actually been worried? For a minute, Bobbie felt elated at the prospect, and yet, she was as confused as ever.

When it felt as if her ass was on fire, she relented. "Okay. I promise. I promise, Clay," she said louder, getting his attention and making him stop.

Never in her life had Bobbie been so embarrassed. She'd never been spanked. Neither parent had ever raised a hand to her. Her father was always too busy to notice if she hadn't been on her best behavior, and her mom had always tried to make up for the fact that her father didn't care one way or another.

Blushing to the roots of her hair, Bobbie glared at Clay as he helped her to her feet. Her bottom was burning, but even that heat was nothing compared to the moisture drenching her panties.

Figures, she thought. *I have sex one damned time and now I'm hooked.* It shocked her to realize she had enjoyed the spanking. A groan slipped from her lips when she recognized exactly how aroused she was. Sure Clay would notice her slip, Bobbie buried her face in her hands and once again prayed the ground would open up and swallow her whole.

There was something magnetic about the powerful man who'd just spanked her. Something deep inside warned her he could easily lead to her downfall.

Chapter Seven

Clay watched Bobbie bury her face in her hands and felt like he'd been hit in the stomach. "Oh hell." He wasn't at all sure what to think. He knew he hadn't really hurt her. He was in control, but there was just something about her slumped shoulders that had him moving forward.

He put his arms around her, burying her face in his chest for a moment until he got himself together. Clay put her slightly away from him and gave a slight tug on the hands still covering her face.

"Don't." The word was muffled through her fingers, but it didn't sound like she was crying.

"Come on, darlin'," he coaxed, then thought maybe goading her would get a better reaction. "It couldn't have been that bad."

He didn't know if that was the wrong thing or the right thing to say, but it didn't really matter because it got her to lower her hands. Her eyes weren't red. As a matter of fact, they were wide and slightly dazed. Her pupils were dilated until the green of her irises were hardly visible.

She looked like a woman who had just been thoroughly loved, not thoroughly spanked.

"Just leave me alone." She stood, glared at him, and walked to where Lady was quietly grazing on some tall grass.

Clay watched as Bobbie mounted alone; she neither asked nor expected a leg up. He winced at the slight gasp she gave when her ass came into contact with the saddle. She just continued glaring until Lady walked up next to him.

"Don't even try to act sorry. And don't you dare tell me it wasn't that bad. If I didn't know better, I'd think you liked acting the bully."

Clay watched her ride away. "And if I didn't know better I'd think you liked being bullied." It might just be a theory he'd have to test out.

By the time Midnight trotted into the stable, Bobbie was already on her way into the house. He'd spent some time thinking. His slower pace would allow Bobbie some time alone to think as well. He needed her again. It had been hours of hell for Clay to stay away from her but it wouldn't be happening any longer.

Clay gave Midnight a quick brush before heading into the house. He either needed a cold shower or time alone to take matters into his own hands. Having Bobbie over his lap, her ass in the palm of his hand, had made him as hard as steel. As he reached the house and the quiet interior of his room, Clay figured he'd have both, the shower and the jerk session, at the same time.

It took him only a moment to gather his things before he padded barefoot down the hall to the bathroom. He thought about Bobbie's room and the huge shower she had access to and wondered what it would be like to shower with her. He might find out later after he got them both good and sweaty from a long bout of mind-numbing sex.

Clay turned on the water, adjusting the knob until the temperature was just the way he liked it, hot. Soon steam was billowing throughout the bathroom, fogging the mirrors, making the room more like a sauna than a bathroom.

Peeling off his clothes, Clay climbed into the shower. Not able to get Bobbie out of his mind, he leaned on the shower wall and grasped the thick length of his cock, imagining what it would be like to see her small, slender fingers wrapped around his engorged sex. To feel the palm of her hand cradle his balls as her lips and tongue worked his cockhead. The vision alone was enough to test his limits.

He would be gentle but stern in her lesson on the way he liked to be touched. After all, she'd been a virgin. She would need some guidance, and from the way she acted in the small office the other day, she would respond well to his patient tutelage. If the wildly aroused look in her eyes after he'd spanked her was any hint, Bobbie would more than likely love being told what to do behind closed doors. He would find out very soon just how far she was willing to be pushed, but Clay had a feeling his soon-to-be wife would love exploring the boundaries of their sexual relationship.

Clay continued to squeeze his throbbing length while rhythmically pumping his hand up and down. The slick feel of soap and water running along his rigid shaft made the pleasure more intense. A tell-tale tingling sensation started at the base of his cock and worked its way into an explosive release that caused his knees to shake. He bit back a groan as he spurted into the warm fall of water. When he was done, Clay finished his shower, then dressed for supper.

When Clay finally made it to the kitchen, Mildred was busy hustling around and Chance was already seated at the table. Clay helped Mildred by bringing the last dish to the table then the three of them sat waiting for several minutes. When Bobbie didn't show, Clay decided to see what was taking her so long. Chance and Mildred both looked at him with worry, but he wasn't sure if their worry was for Bobbie or for himself.

He was halfway up the stairs when Bobbie came flying down them, almost colliding with Clay.

"Whoa," he said as he caught her in his arms.

He felt her stiffen before she turned and moved far enough away so that she was out of his reach. In the process, she ended up a few steps below him, which left him a magnificent view down the front of her blouse.

"Beautiful," he murmured in appreciation, as the full swell of her large breasts strained to be loose of her bra.

She crossed her arms over her chest but the only thing it did was push them higher, making his mouth water in the process.

"Stop that, dammit!" she hissed through clenched teeth. Evidently she didn't like to be ogled. "I'm not some God-damned slab of beef, Clay."

Clay narrowed his eyes, a perfect plan taking shape. "I warned you about your language, Bobbie. You've broken that rule for the last time. Now get down there for supper, Mildred and Chance are waiting on us." Clay gave her a playful swat to her backside as she entered the kitchen, catching her off guard.

"Son of a bit..." she let her words trail off as he caught her gaze. He kept his face impassive, when in actuality he couldn't wait for supper to be over so the lesson could begin.

⁐

The atmosphere during dinner was a bit strained and Bobbie wasn't exactly sure why. She'd apologized to Mildred earlier when she'd finally made it home so she didn't think that was it. Just when she thought the silence would drive her batty, Chance spoke.

"Dad called earlier." He spoke to Clay. "He and Mom are coming home for a visit. He said he'd call tomorrow and let me know when."

Clay didn't say anything. He just nodded and continued to watch Bobbie. His obvious perusal made her uncomfortable. She knew she wasn't the only one at the table who noticed.

"I can't wait to meet them. Mildred has told me so much about them." She gave Mildred a shy smile.

"They're excited to meet you too, Bobbie. I've told them all about you." Bobbie wasn't so sure telling Mr. and Mrs. Bodine all about her was a good thing but said nothing.

"Tomorrow we'll be bringing in a few of the mares who are getting closer to their foaling time. I've already given the boys their jobs so there's no need for you to ride out with us," Chance said to Clay, but Bobbie could have sworn there was an underlying message there. She just wasn't sure what it was.

It was a relief when supper was finally over. Bobbie stealthily made her way to her room. Breathing a sigh of relief, she took out her last lesson package and began work on the assignment. It was hard for Bobbie to believe that she would soon be finished with her course. The thought of taking the final test was intimidating, so Bobbie made herself a promise to study even harder during the week. She also made a mental note to talk to Chance about taking an afternoon off as soon as she got the paperwork notifying her of the testing date.

Twirling her pen, Bobbie couldn't seem to concentrate on her papers tonight. She kept replaying in her mind the erotic spanking Clay had given her. Her body still tingled. She shouldn't have liked being spanked. The whole affair should have scared her, but it hadn't.

Bobbie knew if he came to her, she would relent. Her body was on fire for him, for his touch, the feel of his mouth devouring hers in a need so strong she feared he could seduce her without even trying any more than a crook of his finger.

The thought of Clay's fingers roaming her body made Bobbie's insides quiver. More than anything, she wanted to feel his arms around her, his tongue sweeping her sensitive flesh. The problem was coming to terms with her need of Clay without losing her heart to him.

She was just putting her finished assignments away when there was a knock at the door. Bobbie was so happy to be finished she didn't give thought to who might be on the other side before flinging the door wide.

"Hi, darlin'." Clay gathered her into his arms. He walked her backwards far enough into the room so that he could close and lock the door behind them.

Bobbie glanced at the bedside table and was shocked to see it was close to midnight. She relaxed, knowing they wouldn't be interrupted by Chance or caught by Mildred.

"What are you doing here, Clay?" Her voice was breathless, even to herself. There was no hiding the instantaneous arousal coursing through her body.

"I haven't been able to get you or that naughty mouth of yours out of my mind, darlin'. I'm thinking you and I have something to settle where this is concerned." He dipped his head and nipped her lower lip.

Bobbie immediately remembered what he'd told her on the stairs. Clay didn't like her cursing and as a man of his word, he wouldn't allow her to get away with it again. Her backside tingled in anticipation of what was to come and that made her blush.

Clay released her and walked toward the bed. "Come on over here, Bobbie."

His voice was commanding. It brooked no argument, and although she didn't jump at his bidding, she did do as he asked. Bobbie's body warred with her mind. Anticipation and excitement coursed over her every nerve ending; bringing them to life.

"We're going to try something new. I figured if you learned how to keep that luscious mouth of yours busy, you might not feel the need to say all those nasty words."

Bobbie had no idea what in the world he was talking about, but the heated look in his eyes caused her nipples to peak and her already heated pussy to weep with joy.

"Sit on the edge of the bed and unfasten my pants, baby." Clay's command made her mouth water. It was startling to think she was willing to follow his lead and take his orders as long as it was in privacy.

Her hands shook as she lowered herself to the bed. She could feel his gaze on her breasts as he looked down at her from his towering height. This time, she didn't utter a single word of protest. As long as they were behind closed doors, she had no qualms about him looking at her.

Her fingers fumbled with the button fly of his jeans. She wondered in exasperation why he didn't wear jeans with a zipper, they would be much easier. When her fingers grazed his erection, he rocked his hips forward. Startled, she pulled her hands away.

"Uh-uh, baby." Clay tsked as he grabbed her wrist, pinning her hand against his burgeoning length.

Bobbie took a deep breath, then continued unbuttoning his jeans. Once again, he wore nothing beneath. Bobbie wasn't sure what to do next. She had no idea what he expected. She swallowed past the lump in her throat and tried not to think too much about the exposed penis directly in front of her. An entirely impossible feat considering how badly she wanted to lick the drop of pre-cum off the engorged tip and follow each pulsing vein with her tongue.

When her nerves were a bit more settled, she looked up until her eyes met Clay's.

"You know what I want you to do?" He stared at her so intently Bobbie thought he might be able to see straight inside her.

She nodded. "I...um. I've never done this."

"Done what, Bobbie? Tell me exactly what it is I'm asking for."

She could feel the flaming heat of a blush as it climbed her neck and came to rest on her cheeks. "I've never...um, given a man a blow job before." She felt like she was going to die of embarrassment.

"Not good enough, darlin'. I'm not exactly sure who came up with the term, but there isn't any blowing to it. Now tell me exactly what you think I expect."

Good God! The man was a tyrant, but she would do it because she wanted to taste him even more than she wanted to fuck him.

She released the breath she hadn't realized she'd been holding with a whoosh, causing Clay to chuckle.

"I've never taken a man in my mouth."

"A man's what, Bobbie?" he insisted.

"Clay," she whispered, still a little mortified at the thought of saying exactly what she knew he wanted to hear.

"Now, baby. I want to hear you say it right now."

"Okay dammit." She knew damned well he wouldn't relent until she'd followed his orders to a "T".

"I want the words, Bobbie," Clay stated firmly.

Bobbie sighed in annoyance. "I've never taken a man's penis in my mouth. I've never even given a hand job. There, are you satisfied?"

"Not yet, darlin'. Not yet, but I will be very soon. Tonight you'll do all that and more. And you'll learn to do it just the way I like it."

Chapter Eight

Clay sat next to Bobbie and watched her from the corner of his eye as he removed his boots. When his feet were bare, he stood and turned to face her. "Now help me get these off," he ordered, tugging his jeans down.

Her fingers trembled slightly as she helped remove his jeans and he wondered if he was being too aggressive. He looked down into her wide green eyes as he stepped out of his jeans and he couldn't help but caress her soft cheek. "What if I don't do it right?" Her voice quivered.

"That's what I'm here for." He tangled a hand in her hair and gave a slight tug.

Clay groaned when the tip of Bobbie's pink tongue peeked out to wet her lips. When her cool hands touched his shaft, he thought he'd died and gone to heaven. Then she added the warm wetness of her lips in a tentative kiss. She flicked her tongue on the head of his cock, driving him crazy from the erotic torture.

"Like this?"

"Oh yeah, that's good, baby," Clay coached. "Squeeze a little tighter down low and take the head of my cock in that naughty mouth of yours."

He could tell his words turned her on because she did as he asked with the voracity of a woman tried and true in the art of giving head. Her hand stroked and squeezed the length of his shaft as her mouth worked the head. The sensations were overwhelming "That's good, Bobbie. So good...so good." He growled as he felt her hand tug at his balls.

She gave a little purr in the back of her throat. The animal-like sound vibrated through Clay. It was a purely feminine sound, one that sent him quickly over the edge. "I'm going to come, darlin'. Take me as far back as you can and still be able to swallow."

Bobbie increased her suction, pulling him in deeper and as a result, he came, filling her mouth with his semen in a climax unlike any other he could remember.

"Damn, baby, you're a fast learner," Clay croaked as he sank to his knees in front of her.

He looked up and caught a devilish gleam in her eyes and a saucy smile spreading across her face.

"If that's what you consider punishment, I'm thinking I ought to start hanging out with sailors and truck drivers."

Clay's booming laughter filled the room. "Shh, you'll wake everyone up." Her saucy smile broke into a full grin.

"Brat." He got to his feet, grabbed Bobbie and tossed her on to the center of the bed, straddling her hips. "If that didn't keep your mouth busy enough, I'll find something that will."

He tugged the neckline of her blouse down until it lodged beneath her big, beautiful breasts. The twin mounds were covered only by a thin satiny type of fabric and he could see her dusky nipples clearly.

Dipping his head, Clay sucked first one nipple into his mouth and then the other. The feel of her giving flesh made his mouth water. He continued to tongue and tease Bobbie through her bra until the cloth covering them was wet with his saliva, the fabric transparent. He lapped, nipped and teased until Bobbie's chest heaved with her panting breaths, until she was chanting his name and grinding her hips against him in search of release.

"Sounds like your mouth is busy to me," he taunted as she called out his name.

"Oh, Clay. You've got to do something," she begged.

"I am doing something and I'm going to keep doing more somethings until you can hardly breathe through the excitement. Just when you think you can't handle it anymore, I'm going to make you come until you're hoarse from screaming my name." He stared down at her luscious body. "Maybe you'll remember to watch that sassy mouth." He kissed her quick and hard, then removed every stitch of clothing she had on.

"Stay right there, darlin'." He climbed from the bed and headed toward the bathroom. When Clay found what he was looking for, he quickly made his way back to the bed, the belt of her robe dangling from his hand.

"I think before we go any further, I'd like to try something new." He held out the belt from Bobbie's robe.

"Stretch those arms up here." He pointed to the headboard. "I've got a need to see you tied and at my mercy."

He watched her eyes widen, a bit of worry in them before she did as he asked. A thrill shot through his entire length as he wrapped the soft fabric around her wrists. The fact that she trusted him enough to give up her freedom, if only for a while, was a huge turn-on.

"Clay?" she asked in a shaky voice.

"It's all right, darlin'. When you want me to let you go, just say the word, okay?"

"All right."

Clay started with her feet. He rubbed and flexed them until she relaxed the muscles in her legs a bit. When he nibbled at her arch, she giggled. She did the same when he scraped her big toe with a fingernail.

Her giggles turned to moans of delight as he made his way up her leg to her inner thigh and higher. She was wet and ready but it wasn't enough.

"I want you crazy with arousal, Bobbie, begging for release. When I think you're ready, I'll make you come over and over again before I release you and even then, you'll sleep in my arms where you belong."

"Please fuck me already, Clay. Hard and fast. Please," Bobbie heard herself say as he repeatedly licked her clit. Her climax was just out of reach.

"You going to watch your mouth from now on?" he teased.

Bobbie wanted to scream at him. "Yes. For the love of God, Clay. You're going to kill me."

"Only with pleasure, baby. You'll see."

He lowered his head, burying it between her thighs to suck her clit between his lips. His actions sent her spiraling. The mind-blowing orgasm held at bay for too long shattered her soul into a million pieces before slamming it back together again.

Before she could gather her thoughts, Clay was fishing a foil packet out of his jeans pocket. Once he'd donned the protection, he plunged his entire condom-sheathed length into her wet pussy. Bobbie gasped at the wicked intrusion, which only seemed to spur Clay on. The stiff length of his cock retreated and plowed back into her in a frenzy of lust that soon had Bobbie in the throes of another climax.

Her inner muscles tightened and released as wave after wave of sensation flowed through her body, stealing her breath. Her knees shook as her body spasmed. It seemed to last an eternity and then she felt Clay's shaft swell within her. His movements slowed and with one last thrust, he buried himself deeply. The feel of his cock pulsing within her sent Bobbie rocketing over the edge.

೮ಾ

Bobbie finally roused herself enough to move. Clay was behind her, his large arm wrapped around her, making her feel penned in. It was only then that she noticed her hands were free. Her cheeks flamed when she thought of all she'd said, all she'd done. And now it was morning and Clay was still in her bed. Mildred and Chance would know exactly what was going on between them. She silently cursed herself that she'd ever insisted he move the armoire against the connecting door from his side.

"Clay." She nudged his shoulder. When he didn't budge, she pushed a bit harder. "Get up."

He sat straight up, his hair flattened on one side. Sleep lines marred his face making him look soft and cuddly, adorable.

"What in the hell did you do that for?" he barked, breaking the spell. So much for adorable, Bobbie sighed.

"It's morning and you're still in my room. You need to go."

He narrowed his eyes at her. "Why?"

Bobbie couldn't help but roll her eyes. The man wasn't a dunce so why start acting like one all of a sudden? "Why? What kind of a question is that? You need to leave because this is my room, yours is next door, remember?"

"Don't get smart with me, Bobbie. I know exactly what you're saying, I just don't understand why. We'll be married as soon as my parents make it home, so what does it matter if I stay in the same room with you?"

Bobbie hadn't heard anything after "We'll be married" because her ears started ringing and her hands shook from the shock. She jumped off the bed but realized she was still completely nude. She grabbed her robe off the back of the bathroom door and gave an angry frown when she realized her belt was still tied to the headboard.

"What's wrong with you?" Clay no longer sounded angry but concerned. Bobbie wasn't sure what to say so she tried to play it off.

"If that was a proposal, Clay, you need to practice," she laughed.

"Aw shit, darlin'," he started, but Bobbie quickly held her hand up to stop his words. The last thing she wanted him to do was to give some asinine reason like love for wanting to marry her. They hadn't known each other very long and to be lied to that way would hurt way too much.

"I have no idea what you're thinking." She tried to smile. "But I don't ever plan to marry."

At her words Clay climbed from the bed, still gloriously nude and equally aroused. He took a threatening step toward her, and it took everything in Bobbie not to take a step in retreat. When they were toe to toe, Clay grabbed her by the upper arms and pulled her close. His voice was low, dangerous.

"You may have never planned to marry but that all changed in the stable the other day."

Bobbie swallowed her nervousness. "I don't see how."

"Damn, Bobbie, you were a virgin." He released her and angrily plowed his hand through his wavy brown hair.

"What's that got to do with anything?" Bobbie couldn't understand what had made him so angry. He didn't love her or anything. "As it stands right now, Clay, we're nothing more than fuck buddies." Evidently those weren't the right words to say to him.

Clay grabbed her again, this time he lifted her until they were eye to eye. "Don't ever let me hear you say those words again," he thundered. Bobbie was sure his booming voice could be heard throughout the house.

"It matters because you belong to me. Not for a second will I let you forget it, either." He sat her on her feet and stepped back.

"I belong only to myself." When it appeared as if he would argue, Bobbie stopped him. It was a subject she didn't like talking about, but she felt he was owed some sort of explanation.

"My father was a very strong man, Clay. A lot like you. He kept my mom close, but not because he loved her. I think that might very well have been an emotion he wasn't capable of. No, he kept her close because she was like a prize on his arm. I'm not sure whether he couldn't love us or chose not to, and since their deaths, it doesn't really matter. What does matter is the decision I made long ago to never marry. I'll never go through what my father put my mother and I through."

It was all Bobbie could do to get the words out. Clay was not happy in the least. His mood was evident by the jerky movements he made as he hastily dressed. He had just opened his mouth to say something when Chance yelled from the hallway, making Bobbie jump.

"Clay, Dad's on the phone. He wants to talk to you."

"I'll be right there," Clay called back through the still-closed bedroom door.

"This isn't over, Bobbie. Not by a long shot." Clay swung the door open. It crashed into the wall behind it as Clay stalked out into the hallway.

Bobbie was rooted to the spot, clutching her robe closed when Chance appeared in the doorway. "You all right, Bobbie?" His eyes were full of worry.

Bobbie just shook her head. She wasn't sure what she was, but all right wasn't part of it. "That man is crazy," she whispered as Chance moved closer to her. "He thinks he has to marry me because we...because I..." She couldn't finish. When she realized what she had said, she slapped her hand to her mouth. "Oh God. Somebody shoot me now, please."

Chance just laughed and gave her a brotherly pat on the shoulder. "Get dressed and come on down for breakfast. Things will look better when you've had a good meal and some time to think." As Chance left her room, Bobbie prayed he was right, but knew he was as far from right as possible.

Chapter Nine

Clay spoke with his father on the phone, then showered and dressed. He was angry and tired but most of all, he was impatient. He wanted Bobbie for his own. It was more than just a fling to Clay. He wanted her as his wife. He could picture them living happily ever after. Bobbie beneath him nightly as he slipped his erect length into her tiny sheath. Bobbie above him as he suckled her swaying breasts. Bobbie face down over his lap as he spanked her ass before turning the intended punishment into an erotic journey worth traveling, but she was as stubborn as he was and as evasive as a wispy cloud on a windy day. It drove him completely nuts that she'd wiggled out of his grasp as easily as she had.

He made his way down to the kitchen, angry with himself for caring so much and mad as hell at Bobbie for not caring enough. Chance and Bobbie were sitting at the kitchen table drinking coffee and talking quietly when he walked in.

It made Clay insanely jealous that they grew quiet upon seeing him, but he absolutely wouldn't let them know it. Clay kept his face composed, a mask of indifference on the outside while he silently seethed on the inside. He didn't say a word as he poured himself a cup of coffee and found an empty chair at the table.

He scooted the chair until it was closer to Bobbie and took pleasure at the tiny gasp that escaped her lips as his hand grazed her thigh. She tensed and shot him a look he returned tenfold. He couldn't understand why every other woman on Earth seemed to want to get married and the one woman he wanted didn't want a thing to do with the institution. He'd only brought the subject up once and she had clammed up on him. It was downright aggravating.

"Everything ready for Mom and Dad?" Clay asked Chance.

"Yeah, they should be able to settle right in when they get here," Chance answered.

Bobbie's head swung back and forth like a spectator at a tennis match as she tried to follow their conversation. Clay didn't even know if she knew when his parents were coming. For some reason, that topic also seemed to make her skittish.

"They'll be here the day after tomorrow." The information was for her benefit as well as a reminder to Chance.

"The day after tomorrow?" Bobbie's voice squeaked.

"Yeah, is there a problem?" Clay asked, not understanding why the thought of meeting his parents would make her so nervous.

Bobbie looked from him to Chance, then shook her head. "Nope. No problem. Just wanted to make sure I had the day right."

Clay knew damned well she was lying but he wouldn't call her on it in front of Chance. He was looking for a way to smooth things over with her, not make them rockier. Bobbie excused herself from the table and went to the sink where she started water for washing the dishes. Mildred seemed to pop out of the shadows.

"I've got these. You go ahead and sit back down there and finish your coffee while it's still hot."

The defeated slump of Bobbie's shoulders tore at Clay's heart. "I've got a few things to do in my room. I'll see y'all later."

Bobbie walked from the room. He had an urge to follow her and make sure she didn't clean his desk for him. The last time she'd done him the favor, it had taken him hours to find everything and they'd ended up in a shouting match over it.

Clay was still kicking himself in the ass for calling Bobbie a menace. After all, it wasn't really her fault she stunk when it came to keeping house or anything remotely domestic. The only time she wasn't a klutz was when she was working with the horses. He didn't like the fact that she took on heavy lifting and the like, but she seemed to enjoy it so he would keep his mouth closed.

ဆ

Clay went to bed that night with Bobbie on his mind. He slept fitfully as he was in a constant state of semi-arousal.

The next morning, Clay's need for Bobbie was undeniable. If he didn't get a chance to taste the sweetness of her delectable pussy before his parents' arrival, he would go nuts.

The sun was just peeking out when Clay opened his bedroom door and padded silently to Bobbie's room. He made a mental note to move the armoire blocking the connecting door. He wanted access to the redheaded spitfire all the time. He was going to make his courting of her unforgettable. If she wouldn't marry him after the first offer, he would just wear her down until she said yes. It was that simple.

He let himself into Bobbie's room without knocking, but stopped short when he noticed her bed was empty. The light from the partially open bathroom door illuminated the room, so he checked to see if she was in there but it was empty as well. Worried, Clay made his way back to his bedroom and quickly dressed before heading downstairs to look for Bobbie.

The kitchen was empty, although he knew Mildred was up because something was simmering on the stove. Clay was just grabbing for his hat when he heard a horn honk. He made his way back through the house to the front door, but when he got there all he saw of Bobbie's car were the taillights as they disappeared down the gravel driveway. He noticed movement by the barn and turned to see Chance mounting his horse.

"Chance," Clay called out.

"What's up?" Chance replied, nudging his horse in Clay's direction.

"Where's she off to?" Clay was irritated that he had to ask. Bobbie should have talked to him if she needed something.

"She'll be back tonight sometime," Chance said before he urged his mount to a trot, leaving Clay standing in the early morning light to wonder what the two of them were hiding.

The day seemed to pass more slowly than normal. Clay worked close to the house, keeping an eye out for Bobbie. The horse he was attempting to halter train didn't take kindly to his inattentiveness. After the third go-round between him and the stubborn animal, Clay called it quits. When the sun began to set and Bobbie wasn't home, Clay's worry intensified. In the back of his mind a niggling thought took hold. What if she wasn't coming back? Another hour went by and Clay couldn't get the thought out of his mind. There was only one way to know for sure.

He made his way up the stairs, his heart heavy even as his anger mounted. By the time he got to Bobbie's room all conscious thought was gone. Clay thrust the door to Bobbie's room wide, then stepped inside, leaving it open behind him. He took a deep, calming breath before he made his way to the closet. Clay wasn't sure what he expected but was relieved when he opened the door to find her clothes still there.

It was the same in the bathroom. The counter was cluttered with all the things a woman might find necessary. So where was she? He turned back to the bedroom and noticed a suitcase. It was perched atop the chest of drawers, which was partially hidden behind the open door. With a sinking sensation in the pit of his stomach, Clay walked over to it. It was half packed with clothes. A wave of panic spread over him before it quickly turned to rage. Angrily Clay opened the drawers and wanted to shout at their emptiness. He wasn't sure what to do, but knew damned well he wouldn't leave the subject alone. As soon as Bobbie made it home, she'd have some questions to answer.

He knew exactly what he wanted to do. He wanted to put her things back in the drawers and wait there until Bobbie came back, but he left the clothes where they were. He wanted to lock her in the room and never let her go. Of course he knew that wouldn't work, but he intended to find something that would.

Clay was just about to leave the room when he spotted something sticking out of one of the desk drawers. His curiosity peaked; if he could find any clue on where Bobbie intended to go, he would. He would use any information possible if it would help him keep her on the Lazy B. Just as he opened the drawer he heard a voice behind him.

"Looking for anything in particular, boss?" Bobbie asked, trying with every ounce of her strength to remain calm. It wasn't working.

The man had balls, she had to give him that. He didn't look at all worried that he'd been caught. As a matter of fact, he stared at her as if she had done something wrong. Bobbie squared her shoulders. She promised herself she would not let him intimidate her.

"Where in the hell have you been?" he yelled.

"That's not any of your damned business." She could tell he was pissed but she was beyond caring.

"You are mine," he thundered. "And you work for me, so I have every right to know where you were," he added, when she sucked in a breath at his words.

"I belong to no one." She was pissed that no matter how many times she'd told him that, he couldn't get it through his thick skull that she meant it. "I talked to Chance about taking the day off. If you've got a problem, I suggest you take it up with him."

Bobbie forced herself to stand still as Clay marched across the room to where she stood. His closeness made her knees feel like rubber. His masculine scent filled her nostrils. It was crazy how quickly she'd grown to lov... Bobbie abruptly stopped that train of thought. Where did that come from? She liked him, she lusted after his body even as she bemoaned his attitude, but she wouldn't admit to loving him. To do that would be to fetter herself to a man who was way too much like her father.

"We'll take care of all of that later. What I really want to know is what in the hell you think you're doing with that?"

His voice was laced with menacing anger as he pointed to where her suitcase sat on top of the chest of drawers. Bobbie knew exactly what he'd assumed she was doing, but wasn't going to ease his mind just yet. The jackass had no right rummaging around in her room, even if the room was in his house.

"Packing," she said with a calm she didn't feel.

"Well no shit." His voice dripped with sarcasm. "Why are you packing?"

"To move."

Bobbie gasped when he bent down and lifted her as if she weighed no more than a fluff of cotton. Clay dropped her in a heap in the center of the bed, then straddled her, pinning her arms at her sides with his knees. She wondered if she had gone about the whole thing wrong.

Bobbie didn't know if she was angry or aroused. Probably a bit of both.

"Get the hell off of me!" She struggled to free her arms.

Clay leaned down and nipped her lip, making no effort to soothe the sting with his tongue. "What did I tell you about that mouth, darlin'?"

His voice was husky and his eyes were no longer narrowed in anger but heavy with arousal. His brown eyes had deepened to the color of fine whiskey.

"I'm serious, dammit. Get the hell off of me!" Bobbie wanted to kick his ass. If she could just get her arm loose, she would sock him in the nose and be happy as hell watching his eyes water in pain.

"Not until you tell me where you planned to go."

Bobbie couldn't think with him sitting on her. She could feel his erection as he sat astride her middle. Her mouth first went as dry as dust and then it watered in remembrance of his taste.

"Now, Bobbie. Where in the hell did you plan to go after you finished packing that suitcase?"

"You damned idiot. I was going to move into another room or into the bunkhouse." He just stared at her. Bobbie wanted to laugh. It should have been obvious, but evidently Clay's brain wasn't able to function when his dick was hard.

"I think you're going to have to spell it out for me, baby. Why would you be moving to another room unless it's mine? I won't even talk about the bunkhouse because that isn't going to happen." His voice held an edge of jealousy and possession that made her uncomfortable.

Bobbie allowed a wave of relief to wash over her. She'd been gone today taking her final test and had passed. Once she received her certificate in the mail she was going to talk to Chance to see if he could help her get a job in town. It was the only thing she could think to do. If she stayed on the Lazy B much longer, she'd be trapped. But she couldn't tell Clay any of this yet.

"Your parents will be here. This is their room, right?" She decided it was time to let him off the hook.

His eyes sparkled with mirth as the corners of his mouth turned up. "Yes, but you don't have to move. Mom and Dad always stay in their motor home when they come."

He was getting way too comfortable on top of Bobbie for her peace of mind. "Oh. Well, you should have said something. Now get up so I can unpack."

Bobbie wriggled a little to send her point home but Clay made no move to release her. "I sorta like you just the way you are," he drawled and once again lowered his head.

She braced herself for his assault. Only this time he didn't bite at her mouth. He ate it up, kissing and nibbling until Bobbie was breathless.

"Oh, Clay." She no longer cared that she was pinned beneath him. The feel of his large body warmed hers from the inside out.

Bobbie heard a commotion that sounded as if it were coming from a great distance. But then a strong, unfamiliar voice spoke from the direction of the door, bringing Bobbie quickly out of her lust-induced stupor.

"Damn, son, you weren't born in a barn. Can't you remember to close the door behind you?"

Clay wrenched his lips from Bobbie's, swiveling his head to see who had interrupted him. "Son of a bitch," he muttered under his breath.

She looked but could only see the man's head from where she lay still pinned under Clay. It was enough that she knew who it was. Her face heated as she renewed her struggles.

"Get. Up." Her words were bit out between clenched teeth. "And get out," she hissed as he rolled from his perch atop her, still obviously aroused. Bobbie didn't say a word as she darted for the bathroom.

She might have been completely clothed, but Clay's father had caught them in a humiliating position. Bobbie wasn't sure she'd ever be able to show her face again.

Chapter Ten

The bathroom door slammed, rattling the walls. Clay wasn't sure whether to laugh or cry. His cock was hard and aching and his father was standing at the bedroom door with a wickedly amused twinkle in his eye.

"What in the hell did you do that for?" Clay grumbled.

His father laughed. "Next time you'll remember to close the door, son."

Clay stood, grimacing when his shaft was nearly strangled by the tight fit of his jeans. When he reached the doorway, he was engulfed in a bear hug that stole his breath. William Bodine might have a heart condition that had forced him to slow down, but it hadn't stolen any of his strength.

"Come downstairs and see your mother before she heads up here to see what's keeping us." His father laughed. "I don't think she'd be nearly as understanding as I am."

Clay knew his father was right. His mother, Pearl Bodine, was old-fashioned. It was a good thing she hadn't been the one to happen upon them. Of course, that might have solved all of Clay's problems. He smiled at the thought of his mother insisting Bobbie marry him because she'd seduced him into a compromising position.

Clay laughed aloud.

"What's so funny?"

He shook his head and continued down the stairs to greet his mother. She was beautiful. Pearl was small in stature compared to her husband, but what she lacked in height, she made up for in heart.

"Come here and give your mother a hug, boy," she crooned in her velvety-soft voice as she made her way to him. Despite her age, her movements were as graceful as ever. After the hug, she held him back at arm's length and gave him a long look over.

"You're looking well."

Clay gave silent thanks he'd managed to get his arousal under control before she'd hugged him. "You too, Mom," he said, giving her a kiss on the cheek.

"Now," she started in her no-nonsense voice. "Where is this young woman I've been hearing so much about?"

Clay's father choked and sputtered on his glass of iced tea.

"Um, she's upstairs. I thought you wouldn't be here until tomorrow?" he asked in hopes of changing the subject.

His father answered. "She had me up half the night, she was so excited to see you all, so we decided to head on out."

Clay was happy to see them, but he would have to keep his hands off Bobbie while they were visiting, at least until his parents knew his intentions as far as Bobbie was concerned. That was something he didn't like at all. He didn't want to give her time to build back up her defenses.

"So, what do y'all have planned while you're here?" he asked, hoping he sounded casual.

His dad smirked from where he now sat across the table. His mom, oblivious to the underlying current between the two Bodine men, answered. "Well, Mildred has invited us to a barbeque at her daughter's house while we're here. I think we are playing bingo that night also, so we'll more than likely stay overnight in town. Other than that, I believe we'll be staying right here."

Clay wanted to shout for joy knowing he would soon have a night alone with Bobbie. First he'd have to figure out how to get her out of the bathroom.

They sat at the kitchen table and talked for a while until Mildred announced supper was ready. Bobbie still hadn't made it down. He was beginning to wonder if she was really going to take the coward's way out and hide. He wouldn't let her, of course, but he wondered. He stood and was about to excuse himself to collect her when his mother spoke from behind him.

"I'm going to go let Miss Carlington know supper is ready. You all go ahead and serve yourselves."

With a bit of apprehension, Clay watched his mother climb the stairs. If he knew Bobbie as well as he thought he did, she was going to be ready to rip his head off before morning.

&

A soft knock sounded at Bobbie's door. Her instincts told her it wasn't Clay. The fact that he usually pounded or just barged right in was a dead giveaway as well. She walked slowly across the room, trying to gain some semblance of composure.

She took several deep breaths before opening the door, and found herself face to face with an older woman with short curly brown hair the exact color of Clay's. It was peppered with gray, yet took nothing away from her beauty.

"Mrs. Bodine?" Bobbie inquired, feeling a bit uneasy to be in the woman's room while she stood like a visitor in the hall. "Come in," she added, opening the door wider.

"Why thank you, dear."

Bobbie was at a loss for words and uncomfortable. "I...um...I can move my things if you and Mr. Bodine would like your room back." God, she felt like a stuttering idiot.

"Not necessary, dear. William and I prefer the motor home. Much more private when we've got a hankerin' to be alone." Bobbie was treated to a dimpled smile and a wink. She had no idea what to say.

"So, how did you manage it, Miss Carlington?"

Maggie Casper

"Oh, please, call me Bobbie," she said, then continued at Mrs. Bodine's nod. "I'm afraid I don't understand the question."

"Please feel free to call me Pearl, Bobbie. What I am talking about," Pearl said with a twinkle in her eye, "is how you managed to make my boy fall in love with you."

Bobbie felt her jaw once again open in shock. "I don't know what you're talking about." She hoped and prayed her voice didn't sound as shaky as she felt.

Pearl's boisterous laughter was unexpected. "It's okay, dear. I wasn't sure at first but after seeing Clay just now, I am. It's just something a mother knows and from the look on your face, I'd say the feeling is mutual. My sixth sense tells me you have no intention of hurting my son, so I'll stay out of the situation. Forget I even asked."

Bobbie watched, shell-shocked as Pearl walked back out the door. She hollered back at Bobbie over her shoulder. "Supper's ready and Clay was on his way up to fetch you. If Clay is anything like his father, it'll do you no good to try and hide out in here."

Bobbie buried her face in her hands and took several deep, gulping breaths. There was no way it was true. Men like Clay didn't love women, they hoarded them. Kept them in gilded cages and showed them off when the occasion was right. The rest of the time, they were to act as meek, biddable little women. Bobbie knew the type well. Her father had been one and she had no inclination to fall in love with one.

The only thing Bobbie was sure of was that she was going to have to find her own way in life. In order to do that, she was going to need a job and a place to live other than the Lazy B. The thought was daunting, but every time she considered her options, moving and finding a job was the only one to reoccur.

Bobbie made her way to the kitchen where Pearl Bodine introduced her husband. "Bobbie, this is my husband, William. My sweet William."

Bobbie tried not to blush at the introduction. It was the sweetest thing Bobbie had ever seen. The way Pearl looked at William, love clearly showing in every feature of her face, brought a sheen of moisture to Bobbie's eyes. Their display of love confused her as well. Was it possible to be so completely happy with a man, any man? And was Clay anything like his mother and father?

It was on the tip of Bobbie's tongue to comment on the fact that they had already met in a roundabout sort of way, but she stifled the urge. Throughout supper she watched, fascinated by how the Bodine family, including Mildred, interacted with each other. The meal was nothing like the quiet meals she'd suffered through as a child. Neither was the setting the boring elegance of a room in every child's worst dream. The food was always hearty and edible, the meal based more on family favorites than what was most expensive or looked prettiest on a china plate. Bobbie dug in with relish, enjoying not only the food but the company and conversation as well. Something about having Clay's parents at the table with them helped relax her in a strange sort of way. It was almost as if they diffused the situation between herself and Clay. Or maybe it was simply that their presence almost guaranteed Clay would behave himself.

The kitchen was country through and through, just as it had been since her arrival. The new bright red curtains hanging from the windows gave the room much more color than mere white walls could boast. Shelves high on the wall were cluttered with every imaginable farm animal knick-knack you could think of. Antique kitchen gadgets were laid about, rounding out the overall feel of the room. Bobbie had spent her first few days at the ranch eyeing each and every one of them.

And yet, the huge round table was what caught the eye of most newcomers. It was obviously well made and had seen its share of company. Its surface had lost its high shine and yet it stood proud and uncovered except for the food cluttering the center. Bobbie knew that this kitchen, this home, was the perfect place to raise a family, and felt a small jolt of jealousy over the fact that Clay and not she had been brought up in such a way.

When supper was finished, Bobbie didn't even attempt to help clean the kitchen. The embarrassment of being shooed away would be too much with Pearl in residence. Instead, she made her way up to her room where she changed into a Levi's skirt and blouse. It was payday and she had plans.

She gave her hair a final brush-through and worked her way down the stairs, hoping all the way that Clay was occupied elsewhere. She did a quick search of the house to let someone know where she would be but found no one. Then she heard laughing and talking coming from the direction of the front porch. With jittery nerves, Bobbie made her way to the front door and out to the porch.

"Well, hello there, Miss Carlington. Don't you look nice?" Mr. Bodine greeted her. His hazel eyes, so like Clay's, were smiling.

Before Bobbie could answer, Pearl spoke. "She likes to be called Bobbie, William."

Bobbie's head was still whirling from dinner when Rick jogged up to the porch.

"Hey, Bobbie, I was wondering if I could hitch a ride with you?"

Bobbie avoided looking at Clay.

"Um...sure, no problem."

She watched as Rick greeted everyone else and tried not to show any emotion as Clay strode toward her. "Where were you going?" he asked quietly.

His voice, so low and sure, sent a shiver up her spine. Her body still ached for him and their wrestling match earlier in the afternoon had only made it worse.

"I'm going to the Electric Cowboy with Rick and some of the other hands." Bobbie could tell Clay wanted to protest, but the porch had grown quiet and it seemed every eye was on them. She realized he wasn't yet ready to put himself in the situation of explaining the nature of their relationship to his parents. She was grateful for the respite.

"Be back early, darlin'. It wouldn't be advisable to make me come after you."

It was beyond ridiculous how the man's voice could make her cream her panties even when his words made her want to kick him in the shin. Bobbie narrowed her eyes to show her displeasure, then gave a jerky nod.

She watched as Clay strode to Rick, had a quiet word with him and then began a conversation with Chance as if nothing had happened. She really wanted to scream at him but knew that would accomplish nothing, so she plastered a smile on her face, said her goodbyes and joined Rick.

"Have fun," William said quietly as she and Rick walked to her car. Bobbie looked over her shoulder at his words, noticing how the corner of his mouth tilted slightly. Clay, on the other hand, watched every step she took, his eyes dark and dangerous, his hands clenched into fists. Bobbie climbed into her little red sports car wondering if she was making a huge mistake.

Chapter Eleven

Clay stood on the porch for a few minutes trying to get ahold of his temper. He had never been the jealous type and didn't want to believe that's what was gripping him now, but deep down he knew better.

Bobbie had been home for over twenty minutes and had remained outside. He didn't know how much longer he could wait for her. He was angry and yet he wanted to kiss her silly. Every time he thought he was making headway something would happen and Bobbie would once again begin avoiding him.

Clay tried to push his emotions deep inside but the ugly, green-eyed monster clawing away inside of him kept rearing its head. He needed to figure out what in the hell was going on. This on-again, off-again crap was for the birds. His patience was wearing thin.

Deep inside he wanted to believe their lovemaking meant something to Bobbie. In a way he knew it did. He saw the confusion in her eyes and knew it was part of the reason why she kept trying to avoid him.

He opened the front door and stood in the screened-in doorway watching Bobbie. She and Rick were sitting side by side on the trunk of her car, leaning against the rear window as if they didn't have a care in the world. He could hear their murmuring voices but couldn't make out any actual words.

Bobbie turned and looked straight at him as if some sort of inner radar warned her of his arrival. She sat up and turned to Rick, who climbed off Bobbie's low-slung sports car.

"See you tomorrow." Rick waved as he walked casually to the bunkhouse.

Clay didn't know what he would have done if Rick had attempted a good night kiss. It would have proven disastrous.

A need to feel Bobbie's body against his took over, causing his feet to react before his brain had time to think. With quick, powerful strides, Clay was off the porch and by Bobbie's side in seconds.

"You got something going with him?" he demanded, knowing damned well the question would be taken as a direct challenge. He regretted the words almost as soon as they'd left his mouth. The hurt look in Bobbie's deep green eyes told more than mere words could convey. Her words belied the emotions written clearly on her face.

"And if I did?" she taunted.

"If you did, you'd regret the decision almost as much as Rick." He motioned to where his employee had disappeared into the bunkhouse.

"You know, Clay, I'm not really in the mood for all your macho bullshit, so just knock it off."

He gave her no more time before taking her mouth in a devastating kiss. He wanted her to forget everything but him. He deepened the kiss until her mouth opened beneath his. She tasted warm and sweet, her lips soft and moist against his.

She'd worn a short Levi's skirt, her smooth flesh beckoning him. His hands caressed her bare legs, the curve of her ass. No amount of willpower could tear him from her.

"Come with me." He panted the words against her mouth as he walked her backwards. When she stumbled, he steadied her, then tugged her toward the barn.

"Where are you taking me?" she whispered as they passed the motor home his parents were sleeping in.

She was moving too slow. His cock throbbed to be buried deep inside of her. His mouth watered to taste her sweet depths, to lick and nip her peaked nipples. Swinging her up into his arms, he kissed her deeply, then buried his face in the crook of her neck.

"To the barn...closer," was all he managed before reaching the dark interior of the wooden building.

Mostly used to store feed and hay, it would serve another purpose tonight, Clay thought with a roguish smile on his face. Visions of Bobbie bent over a bale of hay as he took her from behind fluttered through his mind. Clay was so hot, he wasn't sure he was going to make it before he lost control completely. He could already feel moisture against the pulsing tip of his

Maggie Casper

erection. It was going to be fast and hard. He couldn't wait.

Clay strode into the darkened building carrying Bobbie snugly against his chest. He could feel the rapid rise and fall of her chest. Although he couldn't see her face, Clay knew she was aroused, excited. Her reaction pleased him.

Instinctively he moved through the barn until he reached a clearing with several bales of hay, where he lowered Bobbie to her feet.

"Stay here a minute while I find the light." When Bobbie didn't respond, Clay warned, "You move and it'll be your ass, baby." She shivered slightly before she nodded.

A part of him hoped she'd bolt at the first opportunity. His palm longed to turn the flesh of her round ass a nice shade of pink. Then he would be able to kiss and soothe the hurt until she was writhing, begging for release.

Clay moved to the center of the room and found the long string that would turn on the light. He gave it a gentle tug and the single incandescent bulb came to life, showering the large room with an inadequate amount of light.

He wanted to see every inch of her as he took her, but the shadows still lingered. Probably won't matter anyway, Clay decided, realizing it would more than likely be over before it ever really started if the raging erection behind the fly of his jeans had any say in the matter.

Clay was back at Bobbie's side in a matter of seconds. His hands were insistent, persistent as they flowed over her curves. He devoured her mouth with kisses. Her lips, her neck and then down to her cotton-covered breasts.

There was no time for the removal of clothing. Clay had to taste her now. He lifted her blouse and gave a silent thanks to the soul who invented bras which fastened in front. When her large breasts spilled out, he groaned with pure male satisfaction before his mouth greedily closed over a nipple.

It wasn't enough. He pulled her breasts together so he could tease and torture both turgid peaks simultaneously. Her breathing became ragged, the quiet sounds of her arousal increasing until she started chanting his name over and over. Whatever control he was hanging onto was lost in that moment.

In one fluid motion, Clay turned her, facing her away from him, then pulled her shirt down. He placed his hand in the center of her back, guiding her to bend over the bales of hay. Clay was glad Bobbie didn't protest because his need for her was so great he knew he wouldn't be able to give gentle directions.

He fumbled with his pants with one hand while hiking her skirt up with the other. The sight of her bare ass cheeks halted his motion for a second before his hand delivered a stinging smack to Bobbie's backside.

"You wore this to go out with another man?" he growled, not liking the pictures his mind conjured up.

She shook her head and mumbled something about panty lines, then begged for more. His lust-filled mind heard none of it. He pulled his erection free of his pants, then tugged the tiny elastic back of her thong underwear aside. In one swift thrust, he was buried to the hilt inside her.

Bobbie's bottom burned where he'd swatted her. Her other cheek tingled in need of the same treatment. Clay filled her completely. He felt much larger in the position she was in. Automatically she widened her stance and arched her back, accepting him deeper. Her body had taken over, leaving her no choice in the matter but to submit to its will and Clay's.

"Harder, Clay. Oh...fuck," she gasped as he almost completely pulled out; then lunged forward, burying himself again. Bobbie felt every inch of his length as he glided against her vaginal walls. Her muscles clasped him tightly, causing overwhelming friction as every nerve ending was touched, tortured.

"Like that, baby. Just like that," Clay said from behind her.

The coarse hay abraded her sensitive nipples through her shirt. His hands were all over, running over her hips and up her back. Bombarded by sensations from every angle, Bobbie was right on the edge and fighting for more.

"Oh, God," she groaned when his fingers tangled into her hair and gave a quick tug, pulling her head back.

Clay leaned forward, blanketing her body with his, and nipped her neck.

"Not yet, darlin'." Bobbie wasn't sure she would be able to hold out. She was fixing to go flying and was sure no command was going to stop her.

Clay let go of her hair and smacked the other cheek of her bottom, momentarily taking her mind from her impending orgasm. "Not yet, Bobbie." His voice commanded she obey even as his cock and hands pushed her closer to the edge.

He moved his hand from her bottom to the opening of her pussy. She couldn't help but shudder when he touched where his cock filled her so thoroughly. It was too much.

"Now, Clay. Oh God, now."

His fingers played around her moist entrance before moving between the cheeks of her ass. "Not yet," he insisted.

The sensations he aroused in her were intense. When Bobbie felt pressure at the tight bud of her anus, she whimpered and reflexively moved her hips forward.

"Stay still and relax." His voice was low and flowed over her body. The width of his finger invading her caused a bite of pain that sent her into a new realm of sensations. Her mind scrambled to catch up as her body welcomed the intense combination of pleasure and pain. Clay's finger penetrated deeper, increasing the pressure, widening her in slow increments. This time there was no stopping it. A keening cry tore from her lips as her body tightened, then plummeted into an all-consuming climax that left her breathless.

Clay's pounding rhythm didn't let up with her orgasm. Instead, his pace quickened until Bobbie thought she would shatter from the intense sensations coursing through her body. His body arched against her, driving his length impossibly deeper. She felt his muscles stiffen and heard him groan as the warmth of his release filled her.

Chapter Twelve

Clay fixed his clothes. Tucking his now soft shaft back within the confines of his jeans, Clay thought about how much he enjoyed every nuance of Bobbie's body.

"There's no telling when my parents will decide to leave," he said, thinking out loud.

Bobbie turned and looked at him. He could tell she wanted to say something but wasn't quite sure what. Clay remained quiet, waiting to see if his silence would pay off. It did.

"I haven't spent much time with them but they seem great. I can't believe you want them to leave already."

Her words stunned him. Never in a million years would he wish his parents gone. "I don't want them to leave. They came at the perfect time. My mom would never forgive me if I got married without her."

Bobbie's throat worked as she visibly swallowed. Her face was now pale. She finished straightening her clothes with quick and jerky movements. "I told you, I won't marry you, Clay."

"Dammit, Bobbie! I won't argue with you about this any longer. You were a virgin before I took you and made you mine. You will marry me if I have to drag you to the judge."

She shook her head but no words made it through her trembling lips. His frustration mounted and he was afraid he would say or do something regrettable. He wanted to take her in his arms and shake her until she agreed. He longed to tie her to his bed and never release her. Instead, he stalked from the barn, leaving her standing in the shadowy darkness alone.

The night was long and uncomfortable. Clay couldn't get Bobbie out of his mind. Something deep inside warned him that if he spent too much time insisting and no time listening, he was going to lose her.

It was that thought that had him frowning. He wasn't the type to coddle. He said what was on his mind and if you were going to disagree, you'd better have a damned good reason for it. He'd always dated meek, biddable women. Women who listened, not women who lived to give grief.

A woman like Bobbie, who unknowingly tempted him every time he turned around, was enough to drive him mad. Blazing mad with anger for refusing to marry him. Mad with lust from no more than her natural scent.

When Clay didn't hear Bobbie come upstairs, he gave consideration to going back outside to look for her. In his haste, he'd done the unthinkable: he'd left Bobbie alone. Outside. At night.

He threw the covers off his bare legs. He was at his door when he heard soft footsteps in the hall. Opening the door slightly, he made sure it was Bobbie he heard. He breathed a sigh of relief when he saw her disappear into her room, closing the door behind her. He owed her an apology for leaving the way he did. He owed an apology for much more than that but it would have to wait until he'd worked out what he was feeling. She made him so crazy he thought he would go insane. Clay was well aware that his feelings were strong but was it love? It didn't really matter. The main thing was that he talk her into marrying him. His honor insisted, his body demanded.

He would have no peace if he didn't. He needed something tangible to bind them together. Something indisputable that would prove she was his in every way possible.

As sleep crept up on him, Clay wondered why Bobbie was so dead set against marriage. Why wasn't she like other women who wanted nothing more than to marry and have a family and a husband to take care of them?

Why was she so reluctant to marry?

The same questions filtered through his mind over and over as he tossed and turned. The bright light of the morning brought no answers. With his heart still heavy, Clay climbed from the bed and dressed for the day.

Making his way down the stairs, Clay pondered last night's argument. It hadn't actually been an argument. More like a heated discussion, but only because he'd left before it had time to escalate.

He ate his breakfast in silence while thinking over last night's events again. He was going to go find Bobbie and they were going to have a long talk. It was the only thing he could think to do. It wasn't his way, but he'd always prided himself on being fair and if there was something bothering Bobbie, he owed it to her to listen. Then he would once again insist she marry him.

"Where's everyone at?" he asked Mildred as she came into the kitchen.

"Your parents went into town for the day and Bobbie and Chance went out for a ride. They should be back anytime now."

"Thanks for breakfast." Clay took a last swig of his coffee before placing the cup in the sink and strode out the back door. Chance and Bobbie were just riding into the pasture. Sitting astride Lady, Bobbie looked as if she'd been born to ride.

Her back was straight, her hips loose as she moved with the horse. He watched in awe as Lady picked up speed, galloping over the grassy expanse. Bobbie's hair flowed behind her shoulders. She looked like a goddess.

Clay perched a booted foot on the lowest corral slat and leaned over the top, resting his chin on his forearms. She looked exhilarated, happy. He could stand there and watch her all day long.

When she leaned low over Lady's neck and urged the horse on, he held his breath. It was a reckless speed and when Lady's front hooves left the ground, easily clearing the low bar Bobbie had been riding for, Clay almost lost his breakfast.

They landed beautifully, Chance whooping and hollering in the background. Clay couldn't get his ears to stop ringing or his hands to stop shaking. Beating Chance to within an inch of his life sounded almost as good as tanning Bobbie's hide.

Visions of her on the ground beneath the weight of her mount, injured and possibly even dead, scared the shit out of him. Especially when the only thought that kept going through his mind was the fact that they had made mad, passionate love last night. In the barn, over some hay, and he hadn't used any protection.

It hit him like a bolt of lightning, sending his feet crunching over the gravel driveway and into the fenced-off pasture.

She'd been having fun. Of course, the moment she saw Clay, that all changed.

"Speak of the devil," Bobbie muttered, nodding toward Clay. He looked as though a thunderstorm was gathering directly over his head as he strode with power and determination toward her.

How she could have fallen in love with a man like Clay was mindboggling to her. To love a man who wanted nothing more than to own her, just as he owned any other possession, was more hurtful than she could explain. She'd spent the better part of an hour trying to do just that to Chance last night after Clay had left her standing in the barn.

Maggie Casper

Chance was being as nice as possible considering it was his older brother he was plotting against. He had promised to help and, as always, he'd come through for her. Before the house was awake this morning, he'd come to her room to let her know that a few phone calls and a good word later, Bobbie had a job. A real job keeping books for a local storeowner. It wouldn't pay much, but she didn't require much. Everything would turn out just fine.

The best and worst part was that she could start as soon as she was ready. When she remembered how Clay refused to listen, she was ready to leave this minute. But when she remembered the feel of his hands against her skin, his lips against her breasts, she wanted to stay on the Lazy B forever. It really was too bad he couldn't, or wouldn't, compromise.

Bobbie thought about telling Clay how she felt, but wasn't sure it would do any good. He'd proven to be a formidable man and the more run-ins they had, the more she knew she could never live with the man permanently, much less marry him.

He'd already dragged her off of Lady's back once before and Bobbie didn't intend to have a repeat, so she dismounted before he reached her. Chance, who'd just caught up with her, also dismounted.

"That was beautiful," Chance said with vigor.

"No, that was stupid," Clay interrupted, pointing at Bobbie. "You and I are going to talk."

One very large hand wrapped around her wrist in a firm grip. She knew she couldn't break from his grasp, but that didn't stop her from trying. Bobbie dug her heels in and tugged her wrist, wincing at the pain she caused herself. "No, I don't think we are." She was sick and tired of his cavemanish treatment.

"Clay, I don't..." Chance started.

"Stay the hell out of this, Chance," Clay warned. Bobbie was beyond furious, but she wouldn't play one brother against the other.

"It's okay, Chance," Bobbie said.

He gave her a sideways glance but Bobbie just nodded. She was angry and upset, but most of all she was determined not to let Clay have the last word.

Before she could prevent that, Clay gripped her chin between his thumb and forefinger, forcing her to look at him.

His lips were flattened into a grim line, his brown eyes narrowed in anger. He was at the boiling point, but Bobbie couldn't figure out what she'd done to send him over the deep edge. God only knew it didn't take much, but at least all the other times she'd had some idea.

"You'll stay off that damned animal," he growled, causing her mouth to sag open.

"What is wrong with you?"

"Nothing is wrong with me, but there very well might be something going on with you and until I know for sure, you won't ride or work in the stables. Is that clear?"

"Is what clear? What in the hell are you talking about?" Bobbie asked, unable to figure him out.

Clay loosened his grip on Bobbie's wrist. One hand made its way down her shoulder until it rested over the zipper of her tight jeans.

"I didn't use a condom last night, Bobbie. I won't take any chances until we know for sure. In the meantime, I'll speak to the judge about coming out for a small ceremony."

Bobbie's stomach dipped. She felt like the air had been knocked from her lungs. In one breath he could speak of a possible child and in the next make a decision as important as marriage, and yet, never once had he spoken words of love, much less bothered to ask what her feelings were on the matter. The man was insane.

"We didn't use anything the first time either, but you didn't freak out about me riding then." Bobbie could have laughed at the look on Clay's face, but there was nothing funny about the whole thing. The fact that he seemed so surprised caught her off guard. Until that moment, Bobbie hadn't given any consideration to protection or babies. Sex between them had been natural, all-consuming. Being intimate with Clay had just felt right.

Bobbie's mouth went dry at the thought of a baby. What worried her most, though, was the possibility of raising a child in the same type of situation she'd been brought up. A home with a dominant, unloving husband and father. One where the husband was the breadwinner but nothing more.

She couldn't do it. She wouldn't marry a man who felt nothing but lust for her. And wouldn't subject a baby to that environment either. Besides, Bobbie wasn't so sure she'd survive when he got tired of her and set her aside like a forgotten toy, only taking her out when it was convenient.

She clearly remembered the look of dejection on her mother's face after being repeatedly let down by her father. She wouldn't do it. Couldn't do it.

"I'm sorry." She choked on the words as they tore from her throat. "I can't."

Bobbie couldn't stop the tears from flowing freely down her face. Leaving the pasture, she decided there was no choice but to leave as soon as possible or she would be stuck, trapped. If she ended up being pregnant with Clay's child, he would never let her go.

Bobbie made her way into the house, oblivious to the stares she received. She heard Chance's muttered curse as he followed her up the stairs.

"What in the hell..." he started. Bobbie held up her hand to forestall his outburst. She wanted nothing to do with coming between two brothers.

"Don't, Chance. Don't say something you'll regret." Bobbie couldn't stand the thought that she might come between them. They were both fighting for her. One as a lover and one as a brother figure. It was too much.

He took a deep breath and released it, rubbing a hand through his wavy brown hair and down his face where he gave a slight tug to his neatly trimmed moustache.

"I still need to leave, just like I told you. I hate to ask, but I need your help."

Chance considered her words. He nodded and said, "I'll take care of it."

When he turned to leave, Bobbie put a hand on his arm. "How?" she inquired.

"I'm supposed to leave the day after tomorrow to transport some stock. The trip there and back should take the better part of a week. I'll talk Clay into going."

Bobbie knew she looked skeptical. There wasn't much a person could talk Clay Bodine into doing if he didn't want to. "You sure it'll work?" She hated the fact that she was plotting behind Clay's back, with his brother no less.

"I'm sure," was all he said as he left her room, closing the door quietly behind him.

Chapter Thirteen

"I'm not going any damned place." Clay's gaze bore into Chance's.

Clay couldn't imagine what had gotten into Chance. It wasn't like his brother to interfere in his personal matters.

"Would you just calm down and listen for a minute?"

"I don't need to calm down," Clay grumbled. "And I'm done listening."

"Done? I don't believe you. You haven't even started. Damn, man! Don't you get it? You don't listen to a thing she says and you say you're done."

Clay knew Chance was right, but it didn't make the truth any easier to hear. His brother was a persistent man though, and just as determined as Clay. "Take the fucking horses to our buyer, Clay. Take the time to cool off and think. I don't know what in the hell is going on with you two, and I don't want to know, but something has got to give."

For the first time in a very long time, Clay was going to go against his better judgment and take the advice of someone else.

"All right. You win. Just promise me you'll keep an eye out on her while I'm gone."

"I promise. Now go to bed, you've got some packing and planning to do tomorrow."

Clay sat at his desk for another hour before he trudged up the stairs to his room. Something in his chest ached. It was a deep, unrelenting pain he couldn't seem to get rid of. He had a bad feeling about leaving on a business trip right now, but he knew Chance was right.

He'd seen the hurt in Bobbie's eyes. It was clearly visible in the way she carried herself, and he'd done nothing to make it better. In fact he'd only made it worse. Maybe having time to think and giving Bobbie time alone would help. It certainly couldn't hurt.

The only thing he needed to figure out before he left was to find a way to make damned sure Bobbie stayed on the Lazy B while he was gone. He wouldn't put it past her sassy ass to pack up and move out the minute he stepped foot off the Lazy B.

The next day came and went much too quickly. Clay packed and tried to get caught up on some of the bookkeeping. It was a damned nuisance and the fact that he hated crunching numbers with a passion didn't seem to help.

It was getting dark and Bobbie had shied away from the kitchen at suppertime with complaints of a headache.

His parents seemed oblivious that Bobbie was evading him and acted like they had no clue Chance was acting strange too.

Chance had every right to be upset over Clay's treatment of Bobbie up until this point. They would work it out. As brothers they had always been close and Clay had no reason to believe things would ever change.

The more he thought about it, the more he couldn't leave without talking to Bobbie. The need to touch her was overwhelming. His tongue tingled in anticipation for a taste of what she had to offer, but he wouldn't let his body take over, he just wanted to talk.

He could hear her moving about in her room. Clay had moved the armoire blocking the connecting door and decided now would be a good time to use the door. He gave a silent prayer that she wouldn't boot his ass out of the room before he got both feet across the threshold.

He knew he should have knocked the minute he saw the irritated look on her face, but it was the rest of her that had the breath lodged in his chest. She wore only an oversized shirt and a pair of panties.

The shirt barely reached the top of her thighs. Clay could tell she was braless by the way her breasts moved tantalizingly beneath her t-shirt. The sight of her nude legs was making his mouth water at what he knew was hidden between them.

"Did you need something, Clay?"

Her voice was cold, her words curt. He longed to hear her chanting his name as her impending release mounted. The need to change the past swallowed him whole, but Clay knew that was impossible. The only way to make up for the past was by living in the present and giving Bobbie the happy future she deserved.

"I wanted to talk to you before I leave in the morning." He would remain calm if it killed him.

"I don't think that's such a good idea. We've said everything there is to say."

Crossing the room, Clay sat on the edge of the bed. Bobbie sounded tired and sad, making the ache in his chest grow. "No, darlin', we haven't. Come sit by me." He patted the spot beside him on the bed. "I just want to talk," he said, even as his throbbing cock revealed the lie. "We won't do anything you don't want to do."

She relented, moving to the bed to sit beside him. Her body was rigid, not at all the warm and sensuous woman he knew. "That's just it. I want so much that I shouldn't want. It's no good, Clay. We're no good. It just won't work."

He wanted to prove her wrong. To show her how good it could be, how good they could be together. It would be hard but not impossible. He longed to tell her all these things, to show her he could listen. That he would listen, but his body took over. The words would have to come later.

Clay felt Bobbie tremble slightly as his mouth settled over hers. He was consumed with passion for her. Heat burned him from the inside out, but he was determined to take it slow, to taste her and hold her.

He felt Bobbie's tongue peek out tentatively, touching his, and groaned low in his throat. Her taste was sweet, her mouth moist and warm. Her innocence fueled his arousal until he was ready to burst.

"Closer, baby. I've got to feel you."

She leaned in, his words pulling her to him. He cradled her in his arms, the feel of her against him bringing him back to center. It was where she belonged. Why didn't she know that and if she did, why was she fighting it?

Clay slowly lowered to his back, bringing Bobbie down with him. She lay sprawled atop him as he deepened the kiss. Clay grabbed her thighs, spreading her legs wide until she straddled the rigid length of his arousal.

He could feel her heat, the warm moisture of her body as she wiggled to get closer. The thin barrier of her satiny panties did little to deter his wandering hands. He walked his fingers up the back of her thighs and loved the little moan his action elicited.

He continued until he'd reached the waistband of her panties then plunged his hands inside, filling both palms with the warm globes of her ass cheeks. He squeezed and caressed as he continued to plunder her mouth.

It was unnerving how much he could demand from her body and even more so how little control she had over its reaction to his ministrations. She wanted to vehemently deny what she was feeling. She planned on leaving the first chance she got and yet, here she was making love with the very same man she was running from. A wave of guilt swept over her.

When Clay slipped a finger into the tight clasp of her vagina, all thought fled. Feeling took over. Bobbie ground her pelvis against his cotton-clad erection. His boxer briefs did nothing to conceal the state he was in.

Her body tightened. She was on the edge, getting ready to fall over when Clay removed his hands from inside her panties and held her hips immobile. Bobbie whimpered, hating the sound but unable to stop it.

"Clay." She needed to climax. She was so close.

"Not like that, darlin'. I want to be in you. To feel that tight pussy of yours grab on to me and not let go."

His words were crude and should have put her off. Instead, his erotic words pushed her closer to the precipice and in her frantic need she did and said the first thing that came to mind.

"Let's get these off of you, then."

Bobbie had never really taken charge before. She liked the adrenaline rush it gave her. Not to mention the surprised look on Clay's face. She would think of this as a parting gift. To give of herself completely to a man she couldn't admit aloud to loving. It was the best she could do.

She tugged the offending underwear from his body, making sure to touch and tease him as much as possible along the way. When the waistband cleared the bulbous head of his shaft, she leaned forward and bestowed a kiss, using her tongue to lick off the single pearly white drop of pre-cum gathered there.

A smile crossed her lips as he sucked in his breath. She could feel the muscles of his flat stomach contract.

Continuing to work his underwear off, Bobbie crawled from the bed, and when she reached it, stood at the foot removing her clothes. She pulled the shirt up and over her head, freeing her unbound breasts. They felt hot and heavy. Each peaked tip longed to feel his tongue, the heat of his mouth. Even the bite of his teeth as they scraped across each one individually.

Clay moved to help her but Bobbie stopped him.

"Uh-uh, cowboy. You stay right where you are." She wanted to ride him to completion, to feel his shaft buried to the hilt inside of her as she lifted and lowered herself up and down, feeling every inch of him. Clay had never let Bobbie be on top. Her pussy clenched in anticipation.

An overwhelming need to keep things simple infiltrated her mind. She couldn't let things get too deep this time. Their last time. Although she wished she could shout her feelings, she wouldn't dare.

When she was completely naked, Bobbie crawled back onto the bed. She continued moving toward Clay until her breasts were positioned over his mouth, her nipples puckered and ready. He didn't make her wait before bringing them to his mouth.

The feel of his coarse chest hair against her skin tantalized every nerve. The warmth of his abdomen against her nether lips caused her to wriggle in delight.

Clay released her nipple with a wet sucking sound, then pulled her hips, trying to move her.

"I'm the boss this time, Clay, and I want to ride you."

He chuckled at her words. "I don't have a single problem with that, darlin'. I just need to taste you first."

His words sent a shiver up her spine. He had a talented tongue, that was for sure. Bobbie started to swing her leg over him in order to lie down but his large hands on her hips stopped her.

"Just move up, baby." She did as he asked but wasn't at all sure about the position. "Mmm, that's perfect," he murmured against the sensitive flesh of her wet pussy.

The vibration of his rumbling voice was sheer torture. Bobbie felt wanton in a way that she never had before. Looking down, she watched as Clay stroked her folds with his tongue. His hands on her hips allowed her little movement.

She was holding on for dear life to the headboard when Clay said, "Touch yourself, Bobbie. Do it for me."

Bobbie hesitated before she slowly lowered one hand to her breast. Her legs trembled, her thighs tightening around his head as he delved deeper into her with his wondrous tongue.

"Like this?" She plucked a nipple between her fingers.

Her action caused heat to zing straight to her core. She could feel her inner muscles tighten as tiny spasms cascaded through her tight passage.

"Bring one down here, darlin', and part these pretty lips for me so I can taste your cute little clit."

"Oh God," she moaned, embarrassed yet aroused beyond belief.

"Don't be shy. I can taste your release, it's so close. The feel of your body trembling over mine has me on the edge too, but I want you to give it all to me before you take over and ride this cowboy. Come on, Bobbie."

His words were gentle, coaxing, not at all like the commands he usually gave. Bobbie wanted nothing more than to please the both of them so she lowered her hand until she could feel the wet curls covering her clit. She put two fingers to herself, then parted them, drawing her labia away from her swollen bud.

Clay didn't wait, he devoured her, licking and sucking the minute her fingers were in place. It was too much, the feel of her fingers and his mouth, his hands as they held her immobile.

Bobbie came, yelling out her release, as Clay sipped from her, taking all she had to offer. Just as she was coming down he increased his tempo, bringing her to another shattering release. When her body finally finished trembling she didn't know if she could move yet, but then she remembered Clay's lack of release and how she'd wanted to ride him. Her insides heated all over again.

"You taste just like sunshine and woman. My woman," he said when she moved down his body.

She wouldn't let his words get to her or deter her from her plans to leave, so she let that comment slide without saying anything.

When she'd moved low enough to feel the head of his erection prod her, she remembered their two hit-and-miss sessions with no protection.

"Where are your condoms, Clay?"

Clay looked straight into her eyes. He remained quiet for a heartbeat. "In my nightstand drawer."

Bobbie moved quickly to Clay's room where she grabbed a couple of condoms. When she got back to the bed she sheathed his thick length.

When he was completely covered, she mounted him, then straightened, holding herself up on her knees. With one hand she directed him to her entrance, slowly lowering herself until she was flush with his body. "How's that, cowboy?" she asked, her voice husky.

"Fine...wonderful," he amended as she moved slowly up and back down. It was happening again. She could feel the tightness in her body as it gathered heat. Her climax was building.

"I'm not gonna last long." Clay groaned as she kept up her slow pace. She could tell it took the last of his willpower not to grasp her hips and set the pace.

Bobbie lowered herself until her breasts touched his chest and kissed him tenderly, tasting herself on his lips as she did so. "Thank you." She tried to keep her emotions in check and not give away her inner turmoil.

She gave him no time to answer before she raised herself until only the head of his shaft was still inside her. With panting breaths, Bobbie slammed herself down, accepting every blessed inch of him at once. The sensation was a sensory overload but she couldn't stop. Over and over, she lifted herself quickly and then plummeted down onto his cock. They were both mindless with pleasure as they rode the ever-growing wave, only to be tumbled over and swallowed whole by their simultaneous orgasms.

Chapter Fourteen

A persistent buzzing woke Clay up before light the next morning. He cracked an eye open but it was as if he was looking through a haze. The noise wouldn't stop and as he tried to move, he came up against a warm wall of soft flesh.

His body woke up much quicker than his mind had the ability to, and within minutes he was sporting morning wood. The haze was a mass of hair blocking his view and the womanly wall of flesh was a completely nude Bobbie, sleeping comfortably next to him.

Clay cursed himself for allowing his libido to take over last night. He hadn't gotten the chance to talk to Bobbie like he'd planned. And he'd completely forgotten to get a promise from her that she would remain on the Lazy B while he was gone. Instead, they had enjoyed each other's bodies too many times to count.

Clay rearranged Bobbie so he could slide from the bed. He went into his room and turned off his alarm clock. It only took him a few minutes to dress, then he went downstairs to make sure the horses were being loaded and that Rick was ready since he was going with him.

The breakfast Mildred made was flavorless on his tongue compared to the tasty delights Bobbie had gifted him last night. He didn't want to go. It was all planned out, leaving him little choice. He had a bad feeling about the trip and it left him in a dark mood.

Before it was time to go, Clay ascended the stairs and made his way back to Bobbie's room where she was still peacefully sleeping. She might need her sleep but he needed some reassurance.

"Wake up, darlin'." He kissed her cheek.

She grumbled a bit, then snuggled deeper under the blankets. Clay feathered soft kisses across her face until one bleary eye popped open.

"Mornin'." He tried to sound casual. "I'm off and wanted to say goodbye."

Bobbie yawned and turned over. A part of Clay was proud of the fact that he'd worn her out. The other part, however, wanted to shake her awake and make her promise on a stack of Bibles that she would stay put.

Clay chided himself for being so paranoid. He'd go on the trip and come back as quickly as possible. It would give them some time apart to think and when he got back, he'd find out exactly why Bobbie never intended to marry. Then they would be able to work through their problems.

Bobbie's mouth was warm and sweet as he pressed his lips to hers. Her small moan of pleasure aroused him beyond belief, causing his shaft to swell behind the fly of his jeans. Clay knew if he didn't get the hell out of there now, he wasn't likely to go. Leaving her lying there all warm and naked was one of the hardest things he'd ever done.

It took a bit longer to get the last of the horses loaded into the trailer when Clay got back outside. He kept looking toward the house in hopes that Bobbie would wake up and come outside to see him off.

"She'll be just fine," Chance said.

"Don't forget, Chance. You promised." Clay shook his head. "I keep getting the feeling that I'm missing something. Something just doesn't feel right, but I can't put a finger on it."

His father had joined the group preparing the horses and trailer. "Everything will be fine, son," he soothed. "Your mother and I will stay until you've made it back before we decide where to head off to next."

That news made Clay feel a bit better, but the niggling feeling deep inside warned him something was off. He knew he wouldn't feel better until the trip was behind him, which made him anxious to get started.

He hugged Chance and his father and then climbed into the cab of the truck. If he didn't stop worrying it was going to be one hell of a trip. He took one last look at the house before the truck pulled out of the drive and onto the narrow road leading to the highway.

ॐ

Bobbie felt like a cheat as she hid behind the curtain watching the truck and trailer leave the ranch. It had taken nearly everything in her to feign sleep, and even more to not respond to his soft kisses.

After making the bed, she pulled her suitcase from the closet and started to pack. Unshed tears stung her eyes at the thought of leaving the Lazy B. She felt as if she'd been there for a long time but in the scheme of things, her visit had been short. Much too short.

Packed and dressed, Bobbie went downstairs, bypassing the kitchen in favor of the one place in the house where she knew she could be alone. The one place she would feel the closest to Clay.

Bobbie entered the office feeling the same sense of nostalgia she always felt upon entering the dark and masculine room. From the original cattle brand signifying the Lazy B mounted proudly on the wall behind the desk to the newly updated computer system, the room was filled with strength, pride and hope for the future. Bookcases filled with ranching titles, combined with the ledgers scattered across the surface of the oak desk, proved the room was indeed the heart of the Lazy B. Bobbie remembered the first time she had cleaned Clay's desk for him. He'd ranted and raved because he couldn't find a thing. He'd even called her a menace. His words still hurt but in a different way now.

Now they acted as a reminder of exactly how far they'd come. Bobbie wondered if Clay even noticed she still straightened his desk. Of how he'd become so accustomed to her system he no longer cared when she cleaned the room. She'd tried to do it gradually and it had evidently worked because there had been no more shouting matches as a result.

This morning the desk was piled high with papers. Open ledgers scattered the surface as well and for once since being on the Lazy B, Bobbie knew she could do something to help. Something she was good at.

She sat at the desk and began sorting through the ranch paperwork and ledgers with the intent of getting Clay caught up. Several hours later she stood and stretched. She'd finally finished. Clay would come home and not have to worry about playing catch up with ranch business.

Bobbie straightened up the surface of Clay's desk, putting everything where it belonged. When she was done, she made her way out the front door and into the sunshine. Chance was walking toward the house when he spotted her.

"You all right?" It seemed like he was always asking her that question.

"I'm fine. I caught up the books for Clay. I know how much he hates doing it."

Chance nodded, understanding what she was trying to say but had no words for.

"Are you sure about this?"

"Yeah, I have to go, Chance." She felt extremely guilty for backing out on a deal and not giving sufficient notice, but she'd suspected early on that Chance had had other motives for bringing her to the Lazy B than as a housekeeper.

"I'll get your bag. Mr. Cook said you could start tomorrow so that way you'd have time to unpack. He wanted me to remind you that the place behind the store isn't much."

"It's okay, Chance. I don't need much."

If Chance didn't stop being so nice to her she was going to make an ass out of herself and start blubbering like a baby. She was relieved when Chance walked into the house. It gave Bobbie time to compose herself.

She assured herself that keeping the books for Mr. Cook, the owner of the local hardware store, would be the perfect job. The fact that there was a tiny one-room cabin at the far edge of the store property made the job even better.

Chance brought her suitcase out onto the porch where his parents, Mildred and some of the ranch hands had gathered.

"You be sure and visit. Ya hear, missy?"

"I will, Mildred," Bobbie said as the woman hugged her.

Clay's mother, Pearl, seemed confused by the fact that she was leaving the Lazy B. "Clay didn't say a word about you moving," Pearl protested when Chance loaded Bobbie's belongings into the trunk of her car.

Bobbie glanced at William Bodine. He had a stern look about him, as if he might know what she was up to, but he said nothing to convince her to stay. For that, Bobbie was extremely grateful.

"I know, Pearl. I just thought it would be easier this way."

William gave her a reproachful look before warning, "Easier isn't always better, young lady. It might feel easier now, but you'll more than likely be thinking different when Clay gets back." His words were calm and although his tone was no-nonsense, Bobbie knew without a doubt that he cared for her. It seemed weird that Clay's father would give her a second thought when her own father hadn't.

She wondered if it was possible to be with a man such as the Bodine men and not lose yourself. William spoke again, bringing her out of her thoughts. "Now, Chance and I promised Clay we'd keep an eye on you and I mean to keep my promise. If you don't call daily, one of us will drive into town to check on you."

"I will, William." Bobbie brushed his withered cheek lovingly.

Last but not least, Bobbie turned to Chance. "Thank you for everything," she said, her voice full of emotion.

"No problem, Bobbie. I'm just sorry things didn't work out."

"Promise me that when Clay gets back you two won't fight. He'll know and I don't want to be the cause of coming between the two of you."

He gave her a big bear hug. Bobbie wondered why she was drawn to Clay instead of Chance. Why couldn't she find herself in love with an easygoing man instead of one with a backbone of steel?

Chance set her away from him, his eyes boring into hers and she knew that although he was more laid back on the outside didn't mean he was a pushover. In fact, the way he hid his dominant side so well seemed even more dangerous than Clay's in-your-face style.

"Call tonight or it'll be me you deal with, okay?" He smiled as if to soothe the scold.

Bobbie took a deep breath and nodded. "I will," she answered as she climbed into her car.

Chance waited until she buckled up, then closed the door for her. He leaned in the window. "I'll stall him as long as I can when he gets back, but he'll come for you, Bobbie, and there's nothing I can do about it."

Bobbie just stared at him. She wouldn't think about it just yet. She had a week ahead of her to get settled enough so Clay would see she could make it on her own. Surely if he saw she was happy, he wouldn't interfere.

That was what Bobbie told herself over and over as she unpacked her meager belongings. When she got tired of staring at the four bare walls of the tiny cabin, she walked to the hardware store. Mr. Cook was behind the counter. He seemed like a jovial man of undetermined years. He was tall and extremely thin. His glasses were perched on the end of his nose as he squinted at a paper he held in his hand.

"Mr. Cook?" Bobbie asked.

"Yes. And you must be Bobbie. Chance called a couple of hours ago and said I'd probably be seeing you today."

Bobbie thrust a hand forward and was surprised at the strength of the bony hand squeezing hers.

"I thought I'd come see what needs to be done. I can start right away."

"All right," Mr. Cook answered. "Follow me,"

Bobbie did so, following him to the back of the store, through the storeroom, down a hall and into a tiny office. It was neat and clean, just the way Bobbie preferred it.

Mr. Cook went over the books with Bobbie, then left her alone to work. It was apparent after only a few hours of work that Mr. Cook wasn't in need of full-time help. Bobbie wondered how Chance had gotten the man to offer the job in the first place.

She made her way back through the maze to the front of the store. "I'm done, Mr. Cook." She was a bit nervous about bringing up the lack of work but if she didn't, it would be the same as taking advantage of the man.

"I...um...I don't think you need a full-time employee." There, she'd said it. It was always easier just to get things out if at all possible, except for some reason she couldn't do that with Clay. "I can accomplish the same thing working only a couple of hours a day and it would save you a lot of money."

He seemed surprised at her candor but she wouldn't relent. Bobbie was used to working for what she had and she wouldn't take more than she felt like she'd honestly earned. They worked out a schedule. Mr. Cook gave Bobbie the name of a few other local business owners whom she could talk to about some more part-time work. All in all, Bobbie was happy with her day.

It was only after she'd called the Lazy B to check in that she realized exactly how lonely she was and how much she missed Clay. She remembered how skilled he was with his hands, his mouth and his wicked tongue.

It was embarrassing how easy it was for him to ignite her passion. Hell, he wasn't even in the vicinity and she was wet just thinking about him. Bobbie stroked the moist barrier of her panties, imagining it was Clay touching her. She could picture his eyes peeking wickedly over her belly as he buried his tongue deep within her.

Bobbie's thighs began to tremble as she fondled her clit, her hand now buried inside of her panties. Her fingers circled until she thought she would drive herself crazy. All the while, she pictured Clay in her mind. It was his name that was released on a breathy cry as Bobbie climaxed. It took her several minutes to come down from her post-climax high and realize Clay wasn't there.

He wasn't touching her or tasting her and when he realized she'd left the Lazy B, he probably never would again. When physical and emotional exhaustion became too much, Bobbie curled up with a blanket and cried herself to sleep.

When she awoke nauseous the next morning, she passed it off as bad food from the previous night and gave it no more thought. When there was a repeat performance the next morning which seemed to last all day and drain the life right from her, Bobbie's heart sank.

Chapter Fifteen

Clay couldn't contain his excitement as the truck pulled into the drive of the Lazy B. He'd had a week to think about his feelings for Bobbie. A whole damned week to realize what an ass he'd been.

He wasn't willing to give up his dominant ways but he was willing to compromise, and even better than that, he knew he loved Bobbie and he couldn't wait to tell her. Maybe it would make a difference in her vow never to marry.

He thought back over the week and grimaced at the thought of how many times he'd jerked off thinking of Bobbie. He'd become obsessed with seeing her again. His cock throbbed with the need to be buried deep inside the warmth of her pussy. His mouth watered at the thought of torturing her clit with tongue and teeth. It would take everything in him not to fling her over his shoulder and haul her off the minute he walked through the door.

The puppy he'd bought for her wiggled and squirmed on the seat between him and Rick, sensing their excitement. His name was Virgil but Clay had a feeling

Bobbie would be changing it soon enough. He was a cute little critter, all fur and paws, and Bobbie would love him.

Clay parked the truck, letting the ranch hands help Rick unhitch the trailer. He wanted to storm into the house, find Bobbie and never let her go, but he was trying to change and it was urges like those that were the hardest to control.

Clay made his way through the back door and into the kitchen. The house seemed eerily empty. "I'm home," he hollered up the stairs as he searched the lower portion of the house for signs of life.

He couldn't remember whose cars had been parked outside. A premonition coursed over his body, sending him up the stairs in a hurry. He took them two at a time in his haste to reach Bobbie's room but felt her absence before he even opened the door.

Her clothes were gone. Every last personal item had been cleared from the room and it once again stood bare. Clay wasn't sure who or what, but he wanted to kill something, his anger was so great.

He descended the stairs faster than he'd gone up, looking for someone who could tell him where Bobbie was. He'd find her if he had to go through each and every person on the ranch to do it.

When he got to the bottom, he noticed Chance standing with his hat in his hand.

"Where is she?" he demanded.

"She's not here. I'm sorry, Clay, but she packed her stuff and left last week not long after you did." There was only silence then all hell broke loose.

"She left!" Clay thundered. "And you let her?" he added, more as an accusation than a question.

"What choice did I have? It was her decision." Chance clenched his hands into fists. Clay could tell he was trying not to lose his temper, his rigid stance was a dead giveaway. "She's a friend and was an employee, nothing more. I couldn't very well make her stay against her will," he added vehemently.

"You sure the hell could have. And damned well should have! You promised to keep an eye on her," seethed Clay. And then even though he knew he shouldn't, he blurted out, "And she is more than a friend or a damned employee to either of us since she could possibly be carrying your niece or nephew and is going to be my wife."

Chance sputtered and choked, his face going red with anger. Clay didn't care. His fury blinded him and he was already making plans. Right now his top priority was to drag his errant, soon-to-be-wife back home to the ranch where she belonged. And, if she was pregnant, that was exactly what she would become. His wife.

"What in the hell have you done?" Chance asked bluntly.

"If you don't know what I've done that might have gotten Bobbie pregnant, we have a big problem." Not a trace of humor laced Clay's voice.

"You know exactly what I'm talking about. How could you take advantage of Bobbie like that?"

"Take advantage? I didn't take advantage of her" Clay emphasized the word advantage. But in the back of his mind he wasn't even sure if he believed that. Sure, she had been just as willing as he. But he'd known deep down inside that she wasn't very experienced when it came to men. Come to find out, she wasn't experienced at all before him.

"Don't give me that crap, Clay!" It was turning into a shouting match that was getting him nowhere.

Clay gave Chance a withering look. "Don't go getting all high and mighty on me. You brought her here and I know damned well it wasn't to help Mildred. She can't even boil water without fucking up."

"Oh, hell. All right, let's just sit down," Chance said.

Clay stalked into the office, leaving the door open for Chance. He strode around the desk and sank into the big leather office chair. The surface of the desk was much cleaner than he'd left it. As a matter of fact, it was spotless with only a folded piece of paper sitting on top of a closed ledger book in the center. On it was his name. Clay recognized the writing instantly and scrambled to unfold the paper.

Dear Clay,

I know it's not much but it is the one thing I can do without messing up.

Bobbie

He stared at the note in confusion for a minute before it finally dawned on him. He opened the book and skimmed the numbers. Everything was perfectly done. Clay looked up to where Chance was seated across the desk from him.

"Did you know about this? That she could do this?" he asked, not liking the picture he was getting.

"Yes, she's been taking correspondence courses in accounting since she got here. When she took that day off, it was to take a final computerized test. She's certified now." Chance's words were simple but they left Clay reeling. Did he know so little about her that he wouldn't notice something as important as Bobbie furthering her education? He felt like a heel.

"Why didn't she say something?"

Chance looked at him for a minute as if trying to decide on how much to say. "There's a lot she hasn't said, but you haven't wanted to see what she tries so hard to hide. She's in love with you, Clay. It tore her heart out when she left."

"I can't believe this!" Clay growled as he pushed his chair back and stood. He paced the confines of the office like a caged animal. This was information overload. Why hadn't she told him she was in love with him?

What would you have said back?

It was probably for the best that she hadn't, because he would have made a huge mistake by not reciprocating her feelings. At the time he wasn't even aware he felt the same way. But now he was and by God she was going to listen.

"You should have said something," Clay finally said after he got hold of his anger.

"She would have told you had she wanted you to know. It wasn't my place. Besides, I had no idea you two already had a thing going."

"It's not a thing dammit! She's going to be my wife." Clay cursed under his breath then clenched his hands into fists to keep from hitting something.

"Your wife? You keep saying that. Have you bothered mentioning it to Bobbie?" Chance taunted.

"She knows she belongs to me. I've told her as much," Clay countered.

"That's probably why she ran. You know Bobbie doesn't care much for your high-handed macho crap, Clay. So if you're looking to bring her back you had better change tactics, unless you plan on bringing her back kicking and screaming."

Chance was right, at least partly. Bobbie had never liked him telling her what to do but they had finally learned to get along, hadn't they? There was no way he was going to let a woman walk all over him, that was for sure.

He would compromise if that's what it took to have her home with him, then he would just have to figure something out. And if that didn't work, he would bring her back the only other way he knew, kicking and screaming and even bound if need be, but she was coming home.

"Where is she?" Clay asked with a dead calm to his voice.

"What are your plans?" Chance asked.

"To bring her home," Clay answered with a shake of his head, wondering why Chance would ask such a stupid question.

"I'm not sure if I should tell you."

"You damned well will tell me!" Clay demanded, stalking over to where Chance still sat.

"Why should I if you are just going to upset her?"

"I'm not going to upset her. I'm going to bring her home." Trying to stay calm was useless, but at the rate he was going they would end up in a fistfight if he didn't cool off.

"Evidently she doesn't want to be here or she wouldn't have left," Chance added, not giving even an inch to his big brother.

∞

Bobbie's nerves were strung tight. She knew Clay had to be back from his trip by now and she was expecting him to come barging into her tiny cabin any minute. He would throw her over his shoulder and carry her off. Why did that thought intrigue her so much?

It shouldn't make her panties wet to think of him doing such a thing. It should infuriate her.

When he did show up, and she knew he would, would he notice she was losing weight? Would he notice the pallor of her skin? She was going to have to come to terms with the truth before long. The fact that she couldn't keep even water down was starting to worry her. It was getting increasingly hard to get up in the mornings, her fatigue was so severe.

"You doing okay?"

The sultry voice belonged to Lacey Winslow, one of her bosses. Lacey was a masseuse who ran a small shop out of her rented home. She had hired Bobbie on the spot to keep her books because it gave her more time to work with her clients.

"I'm fine. Just battling some type of flu bug." She prayed it turned out to be the truth. "I think I'll go home early today if you don't mind. I'll see you next week."

"No problem. Call if you need something," Lacey said as Bobbie left the house.

Bobbie walked slowly back to her place. The interior of the cabin was cool, making her shiver even though it was a warm and sunny day outside. Her head was pounding, and even though she felt as dry as the desert, Bobbie was afraid to drink anything because it would just start a horrendous bout of dry heaves.

The first thing she noticed was the blinking red light on her answering machine. It had to be either Mac or Chance because no one else knew her number, unless...

Bobbie hit the button.

"Where in the hell are you?" the voice demanded. An impatient sigh followed. "Call me when you get in."

Like hell, Bobbie thought before she stripped out of her clothes and lay on the futon that made up her couch-bed combo. She was asleep within minutes, but didn't wake any more refreshed the next morning.

Bobbie crawled out of bed, dressed, then walked the short distance to Mr. Cook's store where she slumped into the chair behind the desk. Within minutes, the phone rang. It was Clay. His voice made her heart flip flop.

"Bobbie, it's me, Clay."

"Clay" Was all she managed to choke out and then gathered herself enough to ask, "how was your trip?"

"Fine, but I don't want to talk about that now. I was worried about you and called to make sure you were all right."

"I'm fine." Bobbie wished he would leave her alone. He was just making things harder.

"I'm coming by after you get off work. We need to talk."

"No...I mean. I don't think that's such a good idea." Then she added, "And you shouldn't be calling me at work, Clay. I just started and I don't want to get into any trouble."

"I'll be by at six..." he started, only to be cut off.

"No!" Bobbie answered furiously. Was he trying to hurt her? Because forcing her to see him was going to accomplish just that. She needed to stay away from him in order to get over him. *Yeah right, as if that could ever happen,* the tiny voice in her head taunted.

"You don't need to do that. I'll call you when I get home and we can talk," she added when she realized she'd just yelled into the phone.

"Don't argue with me, Bobbie. I can either talk to you in the privacy of your apartment or I can pop in for a visit while you're at work. Either way I'll have my way in this," he stated flatly.

"In this?" Bobbie sputtered. "You mean you don't always get your way?"

"Yes, I guess you could say I do. That would be a good thing for you to remember. Six, then," Clay added before he hung up.

Bobbie was left sitting at her desk holding the phone, her white-knuckled hand shaking with fury. It probably wasn't a good idea to get so angry, but at the moment what was good and what simply was were two completely different things.

Clay Bodine could just go to hell for all she cared, and at six o'clock she would be happy to relay the message to him personally.

Bobbie finished her work, walked back the short distance to her cabin and spent the rest of the afternoon sleeping on the couch. When she woke from her nap, she was so nervous not even her nausea could keep her still.

She proceeded to clean out the tiny refrigerator. There were only a few things that had gone bad since she'd not been able to eat and only one dish needed to be washed.

Bobbie stood at the sink watching out the window while she washed the solitary dish. Clay pulled up right on schedule. He made his way from his truck to the walkway in record time.

As Clay continued up the walkway, Bobbie scrolled her gaze back up that fine body of his to his chiseled features. His mouth was set in a grim line against the unyielding cut of his jaw. She wasn't able to see his eyes due to his hat riding low on his head, but she knew the color well.

Even though it changed often she would still be able to pick those eyes out of a line-up. Whether they were the color of light whiskey or a deep, dark amber, she would know them anywhere. It took her a moment to break the spell he held her in and regain her composure. With a mask of indifference firmly plastered on her face, she strode to the door.

"How have you been, Bobbie?" he asked as soon as she opened the door.

"I'm fine, Clay. It's not as if you haven't seen me in weeks." Her retort was sharp. Bobbie was being a bitch, but could do nothing to stop herself. It hurt too much to see him, so she did whatever it took to get rid of him quickly. Even if that meant he left angry.

"True," he conceded.

She desperately wanted the visit over and done with.

"Why didn't you stay put? Where you belong."

"I belong wherever I want to be, Clay. Not where you think I should be. The sooner we get that straight, the better off we'll both be." Bobbie was well aware she was pushing her luck. She hoped in doing so she would push him enough that he would leave.

She realized that wasn't going to happen when she saw the glint of anger in his eyes and the inflexible line of his clenched jaw.

"Why you little..." was all he got out before he started for her. She took a step back in retreat for each step he took forward. She held up a hand, palm facing out, as if she were trying to ward him off, but it had no effect. He reached her before she could turn and flee.

"I'd like to shake you until your teeth rattle," he growled, grasping her upper arms as if to corroborate what he had just stated. His grip was strong and sure but not painful. She wanted to deny the effect he had on her body, yet his mere touch caused her to tremble. He must have thought the slight tremor of her body was from fear because he muttered an oath and quickly released her.

Bobbie wasn't sure what had made him change his mind. From the angry look on his face, she knew he meant to throttle her and not for the first time, she reminded herself. The remembrance of that day caused her bottom to tingle, heat spread to her core causing it to flood.

Why had he let her go? She wasn't about to ask because he might just change his mind. She watched him run his large, calloused hand through the thickness of his hair in a jerky motion that showed his aggravation.

Not wanting to stay within reach for long, Bobbie backed her way to the other side of the room. She watched, fascinated, as his long, sure strides carried him from one end of the room to the other. He suddenly stopped pacing to glare at her with brows furrowed.

"This place isn't even big enough to pace in. You don't belong here, Bobbie."

She wanted to run and lock herself in the tiny bathroom, but that wouldn't stop Clay from saying whatever he had come to say. Besides, the door was no match for his strength, so she stayed where she was hoping he would leave soon.

Bobbie didn't know how long she'd be able to hold back from telling him everything. How much she loved him even though he made her crazy. How she longed to be held in his strong, capable arms. How often she dreamt about the feel of him buried deep inside of her. How the dreams she had of them tangled together in the sheets of her bed came back nightly, and most importantly, how she was almost sure she was pregnant and how much that scared her. She stifled a sob and turned to look out the window over the kitchen sink, hugging her arms around herself.

Either she moved too quickly, or everything was catching up with her, because the last thing she remembered hearing before small black dots danced before her eyes and blackness descended was Clay's frantic cursing.

Chapter Sixteen

Catching Bobbie before she hit the floor was pure luck. Clay had been keeping a close eye on her, trying to figure out what she was feeling, when all the color drained from her face and her eyes rolled back in her head.

If he hadn't been sure before, he was absolutely positive the moment he picked up her unconscious body and made a mad dash for his truck.

He loved Bobbie Carlington with a passion.

"Hold on, sweetheart," he crooned, trying to remain calm. It wasn't working.

He was frantic with worry as he drove like a bat out of hell to the hospital.

"Bobbie darlin', you hang on." One hand brushed her hair away from her face while the other had a death grip on the steering wheel.

"You're gonna be all right, baby. You have to be because I love you too much to let anything happen to you. Do you hear me, Bobbie? I love you and I want you to be my wife so wake up, baby. I can't lose you. Oh God, I can't lose you."

Clay knew he sounded like an idiot but he had to say the words. Even if she couldn't hear him, he had to say the words out loud. He would never be able to forgive himself if something happened to her and he'd kept his feelings secret.

He stopped the truck with a screeching halt outside the hospital's emergency room entrance then threw it in park without bothering to shut off the engine. Bellowing for help, Clay carried Bobbie through the automatic double doors.

Bobbie was quickly, yet efficiently, taken from his arms and whisked away to an exam room, leaving him nothing to do but pace. The pungent smell of antiseptic hit home, making Clay realize with gut-wrenching certainty where he was and why. When he could no longer stand to wait idly by while they were doing God knows what to Bobbie, Clay barged through the swinging doors and checked each curtained cubicle and room until he was firmly but gently stopped by a stern-looking woman in scrubs.

"May I help you, sir?"

"I'm trying to find Bobbie Carlington."

Her eyes softened and a small smile crossed her lips. "Mr. Bodine, I presume. I was just coming to find you. Right this way, sir."

Clay followed the nurse, wondering the whole way how she knew who he was. At the end of the hall, she motioned him into a room. "I'll be back in a few minutes to check on Miss Carlington. She's been given some

Maggie Casper

medication to help with the nausea. It's made her drowsy."

Clay nodded his understanding, then entered the room. She lay on a narrow bed, her face pale and drawn. Her eyes were closed. IV tubing was attached to her right hand. He moved closer, making no noise. He didn't want to wake her but Bobbie's internal "Clay" radar must have been doing its thing because her eyes fluttered open.

It took her a moment to focus, but when she did a small smile crossed her haggard features. She looked so small, so delicate. Clay stood motionless as Bobbie reached out for him with a slightly shaky hand. It took no more persuasion than that for Clay to move to her side.

She opened her mouth, licked her lips and tried to speak. Her voice was weak and Clay had to lower his head, bringing him closer in order to hear her slurred words.

"I'm sorry," she said before her glazed eyes drifted closed.

Relief washed over Clay as he sat on the edge of Bobbie's bed clutching her hand. She was going to be just fine, she had to be. Easing his grasp a bit, Clay continued to hold Bobbie's hand as he stroked the back of it lovingly. Every once in a while he brushed her hair from her brow just because he needed to touch her.

When the door to Bobbie's room opened and the nurse he'd spoken with walked in, followed by a doctor, Clay tensed.

"Mr. Bodine," the nurse greeted.

Clay was still perplexed at how this woman knew his name when he'd never seen her before.

"Miss Carlington said you wouldn't last out there very long." The doctor chuckled, motioning beyond the closed door.

"I was coming to get you when I found you wandering the hall." Clay felt no need to apologize. He wanted answers.

"What's wrong with Bobbie?" he asked, forgetting all pretenses.

"She's a bit dehydrated, which is why we started the IV. She came around and told us of her severe nausea and the vomiting she's dealt with the past day or so, so we gave her some medication to counteract that. She can go home after some more fluids."

Clay was relieved that she was going to be fine. "Does she have the stomach flu?" They hadn't said what was making her sick.

When the doctor and nurse looked swiftly at each other, it hit Clay what was wrong. What an idiot he was. "She's pregnant." It wasn't a question, so he didn't wait for an answer. "And the baby?" Clay closed his eyes. Oh God, please let the baby be okay. Before that moment, Clay never realized how wonderful the thought of a child was. Or was it just a child with Bobbie that could make his heart beat quicker?

"They are both just fine," the doctor answered. "Miss Carlington will be able to go home in a few hours and except for taking in lots of fluids and small bland meals until her stomach isn't quite so rebellious, she'll have no limitations."

Clay smiled. Bobbie and the baby were fine and he was going to be a father. He shook the doctor's hand and thanked the nurse as they left Bobbie's room. Clay was already making mental preparations to take Bobbie back to the Lazy B. This time she was going to stay for good. She'd be living there as Mrs. Bobbie Bodine. Clay liked the sound of that.

రు

Bobbie could still see the look of fear on Clay's face when he'd first arrived in her room at the hospital. She had also vaguely heard him telling her that he loved her. Begging her to be all right. Her heart hurt not to be able to give him back the words she knew he wanted to hear, but Bobbie wasn't even sure she'd heard Clay right.

She'd been back at the Lazy B for close to a week and in that time, Clay hadn't touched her. No more than a peck on the cheek and it was killing her. He stalked around like an angry bear and then couldn't figure out why in the hell nobody wanted to be around him. It was getting old real quick.

With plenty of fluids, rest, and medication Bobbie was feeling wonderful. She was getting cabin fever but Clay insisted she stay in the house and rest. Today, she was going to push her luck and his limits. She was going to town for a few hours to work.

"I don't think that's such a good idea, missy," Mildred said as Bobbie collected her bag and car keys.

Bobbie tilted her head to the side. "Do you mean to tell me that by going into town to work, sitting at a desk mind you, for a few hours that I'll be putting myself or my baby in jeopardy?"

Mildred gave an indelicate snort. "That's not at all what I'm saying. Good grief, I worked cleaning houses until the day my daughter was born. No, that's not what I mean."

Bobbie felt relieved. She wouldn't do anything to hurt herself or her child but she wasn't the type to sit idle either. It was driving her nuts.

"Well, what did you mean, then?"

Mildred gave her a look then smiled a little wickedly. "I was thinking that Clay won't be liking it much. Then again, maybe he needs to be riled a bit. Get some of the mean outta him. He's about to drive Chance and the boys to drink."

Bobbie laughed. Chance had pretty much told her the same thing. "He'll have to deal with it, Mildred." Bobbie meant every word of it too.

Her trip into town was slower than normal. No longer would she be taking unnecessary risks. She realized she had set herself up for a blowup with Clay but it was inevitable. He'd been spoiling for a fight for days and Bobbie was finally ready to give it to him.

It drove Bobbie insane that Clay refused to touch her. She was so horny, she thought she might explode and although her fingers worked wonders, it wasn't the same.

"Maybe I'll order myself one of those vibrating eggs." It sounded like a wonderful idea. She could have it sent next-day air. She'd be buzzing before she knew it. The thought made her smile.

Bobbie went by Lacey's house first. She knew it wouldn't take more than an hour to get her work done there. She walked up the front walk and knocked on the door.

"Come in," was the muffled reply. Bobbie peeked her head in. Lacey was on the phone so she closed the door softly behind her and collected her supplies.

Bobbie had just sat on the carpeted floor in front of the coffee table to get started when she heard Lacey's raised voice.

"I said no, dammit!"

Lacey's voice escalated to a heated pitch, causing Bobbie to look up, worried.

Lacey shook her head and punctuated her words with her hand.

"I've already told you. I don't have any money for you. We're not together anymore, Andy. Why don't you ask one of your girlfriends if you need a loan?"

Bobbie had heard stories about Lacey's ex-husband. He wasn't a nice man and hadn't bothered to hide his infidelity from the rest of the town, embarrassing Lacey in the process.

"Go fuck yourself!" was Lacey's reply to whatever the man had said and then she swiftly slammed the phone down.

Bobbie stood. "Everything okay?" she asked, not quite knowing how to help.

Lacey ran a trembling hand through her hair and smiled at Bobbie. "I'm fine. Just tired of dealing with that asshole. I'm thinking the idiot speaks a different version of the English language because he sure as hell doesn't understand the word no."

"What man does?" Bobbie quipped as Lacey pulled two glasses from the cupboard.

"Iced tea?"

"Sure," Bobbie answered, forgoing her work.

Over the next few hours the two of them talked and had a good laugh at the expense of Andy Winslow. It was late afternoon when Bobbie finally made her way to Mr. Cook's hardware store.

She groaned loudly when she pulled her car up to the front of the store. Clay was just walking out the front glass door and he didn't look happy.

"Where in the hell have you been?" he thundered, not caring at all that he was loud enough the people across the street could hear him.

"Good afternoon to you too, boss," Bobbie replied. She knew by calling him boss she'd be pushing it, but she was beyond tired of being coddled.

His brown eyes narrowed dangerously and he lowered his voice. It sent shivers up Bobbie's spine to hear him speak so low and calm. It reminded her of the day he'd spanked her under the trees on the Lazy B.

"Don't start that boss crap with me, Bobbie. I'm not in the mood."

"Doesn't seem like you're in the mood for much these days, does it, boss?"

Bobbie didn't even flinch when his arm snaked out, his hand grabbing her around the wrist, tugging her close. "You are supposed to be home, resting."

"I'm tired of resting, Clay. The doctor said the baby and I are fine, that should be enough for you. Now, please let me go so I can finish my work."

His hand tightened. He didn't release her wrist. "I told Mr. Cook you needed to rest a while longer and that you'd be in sometime next week if you were feeling up to it."

Bobbie couldn't believe her ears. The man was too much. "I feel up to it now, Clay. So either you let me go or I scream until half the town comes running. It'll be a big messy scene but at this point I don't really give a fuck. Anything for you to let me go."

Clay dropped her hand as if he'd been burned. He had a look on his face that seemed almost hurt. Bobbie wasn't sure what to think.

His anger mounted and he stepped closer. "We'll talk about this at home."

"Don't do this to me, Clay. If you can't let me be me, I won't come back to the Lazy B." Bobbie's voice broke. He was so overwhelming she couldn't catch her breath.

His hands were fisted, the knuckles white and his jaw was so tense she was surprised he didn't crack a tooth. The tick just below his right eye was new. He was close to blowing a gasket.

He was an imposing man. He towered over her with his broad chest, his eyes dark and stormy and yet, he didn't say a word. Bobbie expected to see a trickle of blood make its way out of his anger-flattened lips. He had to be biting his tongue pretty hard.

Shock would be a mild word explaining how Bobbie felt when Clay stepped back, giving her room. He reached out and stroked her cheek, his head cocked to the side, studying her. His thumb brushed under her eye and she realized then he was wiping her tears away. Tears she hadn't realized she'd shed.

"I'll be at home waiting to talk to you, baby. Please be careful." He leaned in and kissed her lips, lingering for a few minutes over her taste, then he turned and walked away.

Bobbie wanted to run to him, to throw herself in his arms and beg him to understand. His frantic words came back to her. His voice ragged with worry as he told her he loved her and all of a sudden, she longed to hear him speak the words to her while they made love.

The fact that he had backed off and left without putting up a fight proved to her he wasn't like her father.

Sure, he was unbending and unyielding, a man set in his ways, strict and old-fashioned, but he was also gentle and kind and he loved her. Bobbie tingled all over with the knowledge that they might work.

Bobbie knew she was going to have to relent as well and give up the fight. She could learn to take the bad along with the good if Clay would be willing to meet her in the middle on occasion, as he had just then.

Chapter Seventeen

Clay drove back home to the Lazy B with Bobbie on his mind and in his heart. It baffled him how she could seem so delicate and vulnerable and at the same time be strong enough to stand up to him when most men wouldn't.

She wasn't like any woman he'd ever known, which might be why he'd fallen in love with her. As a man, he was always up for a challenge and evidently Bobbie was going to be just that.

He thought back on his morning conversation with Chance after learning from Mildred that Bobbie had gone into town to work.

"Where in the hell are you going in such an all-fired hurry?" Chance asked after Clay almost mowed him down to get out the back door.

"To bring Bobbie home." Clay had looked at Chance as if he'd lost his brain somewhere. To Clay the answer was obvious.

"Damn, Clay, she went to work."

Chance seemed irritated but his mood was nothing on Clay's. "She doesn't need to work, especially not now."

"Why?" Chance asked, his voice going from irritated to worried. "Has something else happened?"

"No, the doctor said she and the baby were just fine. I just happen to think she should be home resting."

Clay snorted, his look going back to irritated. "You keep hounding her and she's going to up and leave. Watch and see if she don't. She's pregnant, Clay, not battling some dreaded disease."

Clay could feel his heart sink at the thought of Bobbie leaving, but he also remembered the helplessness he'd felt when she'd fainted and he had no idea what was wrong, whether she would live or die.

"You didn't see her, Chance. She was so pale and I couldn't do a thing to help." He rubbed his hands through his hair and down his face as if to wipe away the memory. "I was so God-damned scared. I would have sold my soul to the devil in an instant if it would have made her better."

Chance gave him a look, then nodded. "Good."

"What in the sam hill do you mean, good?!" Clay thundered.

"I'm just relieved, is all. For a while there I couldn't figure out whether you actually loved her or if she was just a prized possession."

Clay scowled at Chance's description but remained silent. "She told you about how she grew up, didn't she?"

Clay nodded, affirming that Bobbie had shared her childhood.

Chance's parting words to Clay before he drove his truck into town had been simple. "Give her some room to be herself, Clay, or you won't have to worry about caring for her at all. She'll take that decision right out of your hands."

He remembered vividly the day she had told him about her father, a man who either couldn't love or wouldn't love. The reason didn't really matter anymore.

That conversation with Bobbie was one of the reasons Clay backed down in front of the hardware store. He was afraid if he didn't, he would lose Bobbie and he knew he couldn't survive that.

Clay spent the next couple of hours working in the stables. Pitching hay was always a good way to work out one's frustrations. When he was done with that, he paced the office, coming to a halt when he heard a car pull up. He looked out the window to see Bobbie getting out of her car. He watched with narrowed eyes as she struggled with some grocery bags. He was out the door before he remembered moving.

"Let me have that," he said before he realized what he was doing. Before Bobbie could come back with a tried and true sarcastic remark, he relented. "Just let me help," he said. "Which one is heavier?"

Bobbie handed him the heavier bag of the two, then they walked into the house, Clay following her into the kitchen. For the most part the bags were full of junk food.

Clay gritted his teeth and said nothing, although it killed him to do so.

Bobbie rose onto her toes and planted a sweet kiss on his lips. "Thanks." Clay could feel her warm breath on his neck, smell the mint of her chewing gum. She made his cock harden and throb to life.

"For what, darlin'?" Clay asked, holding her body close, nudging her belly with his growing desire.

"For not saying anything even though I know you wanted to and for offering to help instead of insisting I let you do it."

Her eyes sparkled with unshed tears, making Clay groan. "Don't cry, darlin'," he whispered. Pulling back, he kissed her neck, nuzzling her until she giggled. Satisfied she wasn't crying any longer, he set her away from him. "I might spend a lot of time being an ass and I might be high-handed and bossy but I love you, Bobbie. More than you'll ever know."

Clay watched as her eyes once again filled, this time spilling over to wet her cheeks. She was laughing and nodding. "Sometimes you are an ass and I know better than most how high-handed you can be and as long as you don't mind a good argument every now and then to work out our differences, I think those are traits I can learn to deal with." Bobbie launched herself at Clay and when he held her tight around the waist, she encircled his neck with her arms and kissed him full on the mouth.

"I love you, Clay," she murmured against his mouth. "I love you so much I can't stand it."

છ

Clay carried Bobbie to their room and snuggled with her under the covers. It might have only been hours since Clay had admitted to loving her, but it had been days since he'd made love to her. She was going to go plumb nuts if something didn't happen soon.

They slept side by side every night, Clay holding her in his arms but going no further. He would tease and caress but that was as far as he'd go.

"Clay," Bobbie whispered wiggling her bottom against his lap.

He groaned. "Go to sleep, sweetheart." He was trying to sound firm but it wasn't working.

"Do you really love me?"

Clay levered himself up on an elbow to look over her shoulder into her face. Even in the shadowed darkness, Bobbie could see his eyes. His feelings for her were evident in the whiskey-brown orbs.

"You know I do, darlin'. Haven't I told you over and over in the past few hours?"

Bobbie pouted, then giggled as Clay leaned in and sucked her outthrust bottom lip. Her giggle turned into a stifled moan as the warmth of his wet mouth tugging on her lip sent a jolt of electricity straight to her pussy, causing it to flood and spasm.

"You told me and I loved hearing it, Clay, but I want you to show me." He grumbled and groaned, making

Bobbie feel bad. Maybe he wouldn't sleep with her now that she was pregnant. Maybe he found her body offensive, even though the only thing different Bobbie had noticed was an increased sensitivity in her breasts.

She sighed and turned back to a position where she was lying on her side hoping to hide the stream of tears coursing down her cheek. It didn't work.

"What is it, baby? Are you feeling sick again?" He was already reaching for the phone.

"No, Clay, I'm not sick. Nothing's wrong. I guess I'm just emotional."

"You sure?"

"Yeah," she hiccoughed. "I'm sure."

"Dammit," Clay raged, rolling her onto her back. "If something is wrong, you'd better tell me."

The sound of his voice, so sure and strong, so demanding, made her insides quiver and heat. Bobbie arched against him needing to feel the warmth of his body against hers.

"I just need you to make love to me."

Bobbie was disappointed when Clay rolled her back onto her side. She was completely naked and so was he. Clay snuggled up behind her, and she felt the tell-tale bulge of his erection at her lower back.

One muscular arm snaked around her waist, then lower until her sex was cradled in the palm of his hand. He toyed with her for a minute, running his fingers along her slit. He dipped in just enough to make her pant and writhe against him before his hand strayed to her thigh. He lifted her leg until it rested at an angle over his hip, leaving her exposed.

"You sure?" His voice was a husky murmur at her ear.

"Hell yeah, I'm sure," Bobbie said, leading one of Clay's hands to her breast. The taut peak was just begging for attention.

Clay chuckled. He tweaked and plucked her nipple with one hand as he stroked the length of his shaft into her from behind. He used his other hand to play with her clit until she gasped with pleasure.

"Oh fuck." Bobbie couldn't help the words as they tumbled from her mouth. Her body was tight, welcoming the impending orgasm as it began to ripple through her muscles.

"That mouth, darlin'. I thought we'd taken care of that," he said, his breath hot against her neck as he increased his tempo. The sounds of their sex filled the otherwise silent room. She didn't understand it, but the lewd noises turned her on even more and before she knew it, she was adding to them by moaning and panting with each stroke of his cock as he buried it completely within her.

The position he held her in was wonderful. Bobbie could feel Clay's penis as it filled her. She could feel each ridge and vein as he throbbed within her, rubbing the tiny bundle of nerves from within.

"Harder, Clay. Fuck me harder," she panted through her orgasm, using language that wasn't at all normal for her. Something in the back of her mind hoped her use of such foul language would result in Clay's version of punishment for the offense. Her mouth watered at the thought. When she could once again breathe freely, Bobbie decided to push her luck just a bit.

"Holy shit!" she exclaimed. "That was beyond fucking great."

Clay hooted in laughter from behind her just before the sound of flesh smacking flesh filled the room. Blazing heat soon streaked across her backside and just like that, Bobbie was hot again.

"I'm thinking you need a reminder of what happens when you can't curb your tongue, darlin'."

Clay sat beside her on the bed, gloriously nude and ready. Bobbie batted her eyes in what she hoped resembled an innocent gesture. "You think so, cowboy?" she taunted.

"I know so," he said, lying down until he was flat on his back, his head elevated on a single pillow, hands clasped behind him. He watched her with pure sensual heat flashing from his eyes as she crawled down his body.

When she reached the apex of his thighs, where his jutting arousal stood proud, Bobbie looked up with a wicked smile.

"Then...remind me," she said.

And he did.

Epilogue

The wedding went off without a hitch. Bobbie looked magical as she walked up the grass aisle to her groom. The weather was perfect for an outdoor wedding. The sky was blue with white fluffy clouds dotting it, the scent of roses wafting on the breeze.

Chance listened intently as his brother and Bobbie exchanged their vows, but his eyes were trained elsewhere. The woman he watched belonged to him, she just didn't know it yet.

Lacey Winslow was a tiny woman with a heart of gold. She was also a married woman. Soon to be divorced, Chance reminded himself. She'd been married to the biggest ass in California. There had been many times when Chance had wanted to kill the man with his bare hands, but it wouldn't have won Lacey. So as long as she wasn't being hurt, Chance stayed on the sidelines.

Now that Mr. Lacey was out of the picture though, the little blonde pixie was his. He'd told her as much at her home office just a few days ago. That hadn't gone over quite the way he'd planned, but Chance Bodine wasn't one to give up.

The thought of Lacey with her tiny, delicate hands massaging anyone besides him was enough to drive him crazy. The fact that she'd been setting up an appointment with one of the local muscle-bound firefighters when he'd gone to visit had almost pushed him too far.

He'd waited long enough for her and now it was time to collect. Watching the woman dance with some of the wedding guests was enough to tighten his hands into fists. She had a smile for everyone but him, and that smile was lethal. Her dimples should be outlawed, as well as the rest of her compact little body.

Chance groaned as his cock hardened. He stayed that way when Lacey was around. He was so hard he could drive a fence post with no tools other than his shaft. What he really wanted to drive was the full length of his cock into her over and over again. The urge to drag her behind the barn and ride her tiny, perfect body was overwhelming. It was a desire that continued to consume him. One there was no need to consider further. The wicked thought crossed his mind as he walked around the dance floor in his loose-legged, rolling-hipped cowboy way. His tan Stetson rode low on his head, shielding the lust in his eyes from the crowd at large. He'd save the promise in his heated gaze for Lacey Winslow alone.

About the Author

To learn more about Maggie Casper, please visit www.maggiecasper.com. Send an email to Maggie Casper at maggie@maggiecasper.com or join her Yahoo! group to join in the fun with other readers as well as Maggie Casper! http://groups.yahoo.com/group/sultrysiren.

Look for these titles by
Maggie Casper

Now Available:

Something Old, Something New
Teaching Elena
Every Beat of Her Heart
For the Love of Callie
Knotty Girl ~ A Midsummer Night's Steam book

Will revenge tear them apart, or will Mica do anything for the love of Callie?

For the Love of Callie
© 2007 Maggie Casper

Revenge is sweeter than life itself. So think fools. And so thought Mica Blackfeather. The plan was simple. To take from Callie Jones what she had taken from him. His home and his love.

Callie Jones didn't think things could get any worse. She had no family left and no way to save her home. But when Mica Blackfeather blackmails her into becoming his wife in order to save her home, could she refuse?

Can past wrongs be made right? Will Mica's revenge tear him and Callie apart? Or will it be Mica who will do anything for the love of Callie?

This book has been previously published.

Available now in ebook from Samhain Publishing.

Enjoy the following excerpt For the Love of Callie…

"What now, Callie?" He tried to keep his voice even, but he was running low on patience.

A look of determination crossed her face just before she slid her hand from beneath his, and clasped it tightly in her lap. "Who would you invite?" she asked.

"Well, pretty much everyone. I mean, you mention it to a few but everyone shows up. You know how it works out here, Callie."

"I don't think this is a good idea."

Damn, he was trying to be the good guy, and the fool woman was being difficult.

"It doesn't matter, Callie. We'll go into town tomorrow for supplies and some new clothes. That'll give us the chance to pass the word around."

He wasn't going to leave her a choice in the matter. She was wearing clothes better suited as rags and hadn't seen a soul except for the people she worked with since he'd married her.

Trying to ignore the flush of her face, his dread warred with anger. He wasn't sure why, so he ate his dinner then excused himself from the table. He needed some time to think. It probably wouldn't make a difference though, because he'd never figure the stubborn woman out.

As he headed toward the front door and the solitude of the porch, he heard soft voices along with the occasional clatter of the dishes as they were washed.

"I'm sorry I ruined your dinner," Callie said, her voice morose.

"No need to apologize, Callie. But I must admit that I'm quite confused as to why you wouldn't want someone besides me to visit with."

"It's not that, Delia," she started. Mica knew it was wrong to listen in on their conversation, especially since he'd just chastised Callie for doing the same thing, but he couldn't help himself.

"I've been alone for a long time. Except for Max, I haven't really had any friends for more years than I can remember. I was embarrassed to bring them home." The last was said in a voice so low that Mica moved closer to the door so he'd be able to hear.

"Callie, it wasn't your fault, you know that don't you? What your mother made of herself after your father's death had nothing to do with you."

"But don't you see, Delia? A lot of people don't understand. They don't know how I covered for her. Not to save her from others knowing, but to save others from her."

"I can feel your pain, Callie. It blooms bright in your chest, but your mother is gone now. Why don't you explain it to those you think you've hurt?

"I can't," was the sobbed reply. It tore at his heart to hear the hurt in her voice. The tremble of the words as they were forced out proved this was something she never talked about.

"Then tell me, Callie. Maybe once you've talked about it, your burdens will lessen."

"Thank you, Delia, but there's no use in reliving it all. Besides, it's only part of the problem."

Her voice was a bit stronger now. He could mentally picture how her shoulders had squared, her stubborn chin lifted. Her hands would give her away though. They were probably balled into white-knuckled fists. Her next words were like a punch to the stomach, knocking the breath from his lungs.

"They were there. They'll all know."

"Know what, Callie?" His mother sounded completely bewildered which didn't happen often. Damn! He wished he could see her face, wished it was him that she was telling her fears to.

"They not only know that Mica owns my ranch, but they were there when we married in front of that skunk of a judge, so they know he owns me as well. People shouldn't be owned, Delia. It's not right." Her voice was tortured and sounded far away as his brain tried to sort through her words.

"Then they also know you were given no choice. You've nothing to be embarrassed about. Nothing at all."

"We all have choices, Delia, and I made mine. I chose to marry a man who hates me to save a piece of land I'll never own, and a home I've spent my whole life miserable in. And, I did it in tattered clothes stained in blood in front of half the town." Her laugh was mocking, mirthless. He felt physically ill. Hearing it from her point of view gave him a whole new outlook. "I don't wear his ring, or carry his love in here," she said. He could imagine her hand resting over her heart. "I work his land and warm his bed, Delia, nothing more. A ranch hand and a whore could accomplish the same thing. Makes me wonder which I am?"

Her parting words made him want to roar, but before he had the chance to do anything the kitchen door swung open and out ran Callie.

She halted in her tracks when she saw him, then wiped the tears streaming from her desolate green eyes and continued for the front door.

He was so shocked he just stood there. He couldn't seem to move a muscle. It took a nudge from his mother to get him moving, but it was too late. She'd already saddled up Little Girl and ridden off.

CPSIA information can be obtained at www.ICGtesting.com
Printed in the USA
236966LV00001B/66/P